Salt & Sunshine

MINDY PAIGE

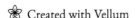

Salt & Sunshine

Cassandra Stone is in a rut. It's been a year since she got kicked out of her dream school in Paris. Twelve months since she returned to her dead-end job and the life she tried so hard to escape. But only one day since she found out her boyfriend cheated on her.

Desperate to cheer her up, her best friend signs them up for a drawing class. What she doesn't mention is that the model is nude. Or that he happens to be her childhood best friend, Jace Maddox.

Except he's not the same Jace. It's been a few years since they last spoke, and he's all grown up, muscular, and mouth-wateringly gorgeous. Oh, and apparently he's a billionaire set out to save the world.

Now, she just has to hope he doesn't hold a grudge for the way they left things. That, and pray these newfound feelings don't ruin their friendship for good.

Chapter One

WHEN NORMAL PEOPLE FIND THEIR BOYFRIEND on a hookup app, I doubt their first thought is to set up an elaborate catfishing scheme to catch them in the act.

Then again, no one has ever described me as normal.

A sigh brushes my lips as I twist the chain of my necklace around my finger. I press the pad of my thumb against one of the six points of the golden sun, focusing on the sharp sting rather than the gentle tremble in my knees.

"You ready?"

I watch my best friend fluff the edges of her platinum blond bob, wishing I had an ounce of her composure. When I first found out Chaz cheated, I was ready to raise hell. Now, all that anger has filtered into a quiet acceptance. Mostly, what I feel is... tired.

"As I'll ever be," I mutter, stepping back from the counter. I tug at the edges of the slinky black dress Kasey loaned me, willing it to turn into a pair of sweats.

"I can't wait to see the look on that asshole's face when you walk up to him," Kasey chirps, her crystal eyes shining mischievously. "He's gonna have no clue what hit him."

Kasey's the one who found his profile on K!nkF!nder, and when I told her about my plan to catch him in the act, she jumped in wholeheartedly. It's ironic that *she's* the one pushing this forward now, when all I want to do is curl up in bed with a pint of cookie dough.

I'm about to voice this to her when my phone buzzes. Heat creeps up the back of my neck and fills my head with a loud, swooshing sound as I read the message.

CHAZ

What's taking so long, sexy? 😏
Waiting for you at the table.

Kasey quirks a brow, letting me know my expression can't be pleasant. I turn the phone toward her, and her nose scrunches in disgust.

2

"That dickless worm! Do you want me to go outside and key his car?"

"That won't be necessary." I give her a stern look.

"Fine. Sugar in the gas tank?"

"No!" I narrow my eyes. "We're not doing anything that could land you in prison, Kase."

"Fine. But the offer will be there when you change your mind."

I roll my eyes, taking one last glance at my reflection to steel myself. "How do I look?"

"Hot as hell," Kasey affirms, giving me a flirtatious once-over. "Go get 'em!" she cheers, swatting my ass lightly as I turn for the exit.

My stilettos click seductively against the tile as I make my leave, filling my chest with a sense of confidence. That is, until one misplaced step sends me lurching to the side.

"Maybe the heels weren't such a great idea," I grumble, attempting to steady myself.

Kasey narrows her eyes as she stalks over to me. "You. Look. Hot. Now get out there!" she orders, placing her hands on my bare back and shoving me toward the door.

My eyes fight to acclimate to the lack of lighting as I step into the dining room of Elevage. Plastic botanicals and fine cloth napkins line each seating arrangement, adding to the guise of a fine dining restaurant.

The perfect place to take a cheap date you want to impress.

A mousy-haired server catches my eye and jerks her head toward a secluded corner booth. I don't know how she knows, but I assume it has something to do with Kasey. Time slows as a strange mixture of rage and heartache fills my veins, crowding my vision with red as I stomp over to my cheating worm of a boyfriend.

A server hurries to a table on my left, balancing a large tray of drinks atop his shoulder. Without pause, I snatch a glass from the outside row, deaf to his cries of protest as a high-pitched ringing fills my ears.

I spin on my heels, taking exactly three steps in the direction of Chaz's booth. He looks up expectantly, pushing his sunglasses to his forehead with a dopey smile. It's only in place for a moment, and my chest pings with satisfaction as his crystalline eyes flash with alarm.

"Cassie? What are you doing h—"

Gasps of shock ring out as the contents of the drink splash on his face.

"W-What the *hell* was that for?" he sputters, the contents dripping onto the collar of his salmon-colored button-down.

I cock my head. "Didn't I get you that shirt for our anniversary?"

"What?" he blubbers.

"Damn... that was pretty expensive too," I murmur. Turning on my heels, I shove my hand into some poor man's spaghetti, numb to the blistering heat as I fist the slimy noodles and whirl back toward Chaz. With the eyes of the entire dining room on my back, I hurl the steaming ball of pasta at his chest. Red sauce splatters his neck and flies up his nose, causing him to choke as he springs from his seat.

"Shit!" he yelps, wiping furiously at the blistering sauce coating his skin. "What the *fuck*, Cassie?"

I flutter my lashes innocently. "Oh, I'm sorry. Were you expecting a warm welcome even though you're literally sitting here about to *cheat* on me?

The color drains from his face.

"Whoever told you that is *lying,* Cass! I wouldn't do that to you, I wouldn't!" He takes a step toward me.

"You absolute public toilet seat of a man." I pinch the bridge of my nose. "You do realize that *I'm* Jessica, right? From K!nkF!nder?"

He gives me a dumbfounded look. "You... you fucking *catfished* me?"

I roll my eyes. "It sure seems that way, doesn't it?" *Thank God I never slept with him. Our kids would have been morons.*

"Cassie, you have to understand. I've tried to be

patient, to wait until you're ready. But it's been a year! Men have *urges*, you have to understa—"

Not the least bit interested in the rest of that statement, I turn on my heel and saunter toward the exit, my hips swinging side to side with each powerful step. The eyes of the entire dining room follow me out, but my adrenaline surges too hard for me to pay them any mind.

"Oh my *God*, that was amazing!" Kasey whispers excitedly. "I swear you could hear a *pin* drop in the place!"

"Oh, *fantastic*," I grumble as I follow her outside. "I'm sure they all thought I was a psycho."

"Au contraire, my friend." Kasey grins, throwing an arm over my shoulder. "That spaghetti splatter was impressive. A couple of those ladies were ready to give you a standing ovation just for that."

I rest my ear on her shoulder, letting out a tired laugh. "Thanks, Kase," I say, my voice welling with emotion. "I don't know how I would have gotten through tonight without you."

"Puh-lease. You'll be over 'Great Value' Mr. Potato Head in no time. In fact..." She brings a finger to her chin. "I'm making it my personal mission to find you a guy to get under so you can get *over* your shitty ex."

My mouth pops open, but Kasey spots something

over my shoulder before a word of protest can leave my lips.

"Speak of the devil," she mutters, her nose scrunched in disgust. "Don't look now, but the ex in question is making a beeline over here. And he doesn't look happy."

Immediately, my head snaps over my shoulder.

"Cass! I told you not to look!" Kasey groans, smacking her forehead. "Now he's walking faster. Great."

"Cassandra!" Chaz's annoying whine calls across the parking lot. "I know you can hear me! Just wait there, let me explain!"

"Not a chance, dinky dick!" Kasey calls back, each word dripping with venom. "Go climb back into whichever pit of hell you came from and leave my best friend alone!"

"Kase!" I gasp, clapping a hand to my mouth to suppress a giggle

Without a word, she grips my upper arm and pulls me over to the passenger side of the car. "Get in! We gotta go before he catches up!" She shoves me inside with surprising strength and rushes to the driver's side of her neon pink Mustang.

"We're off!" she cheers, revving the engine before shifting gears and peeling out of the parking space.

Instead of heading for the exit, though, she circles the lot and speeds back toward Chaz.

"What are you doing?" I throw my arms in the air. "I thought the point was to get away?"

"Just hold on. I have a feeling you'll like this," she promises, her lips creeping into a devious grin. Kasey reaches into the cupholder by her feet and pulls out a plastic cup filled with a horrendous brown sludge.

"Jesus Christ!" I cry, shifting as far away from the abomination as possible. "What is that, and how long has it been in here?"

Kasey pauses for a moment. "Coffee, I think? And you know what...? I actually don't know how long," she says, shrugging it off like she hasn't been riding around with a biological weapon.

The tires screech angrily as Kasey stops in front of a spaghetti-covered Chaz. Rolling down the window, she pokes her head out with an innocent smile.

"Hey, dickbag! I got a present for you!"

In slow motion, the sludge flies through the air in a perfect arc, covering Chaz's face and chest. As soon as the contents land, he doubles over in a dry heave, the smell and taste too much to bear. Even I feel a little sick.

"Consider it a parting gift!" Kasey screams, then peels off before he has time to recover. A giggle bubbles in my chest when I look in the rearview mirror.

"That was possibly one of the coolest things I've seen you do."

"Don't you mean gross?" she asks, a satisfied smirk growing on her face.

"Oh God, *so gross.*" I giggle, unable to hold it in any longer. "But it was also pretty awesome."

"Well, *I'm* pretty awesome, so…"

"You're a dork." I laugh, swatting her arm. "Seriously, though. Thank you, Kase. You made me feel like I can get through this."

"Don't thank me yet." She winks. "Not until I find you a new boy toy."

"Are we still doing that?" I groan, letting my forehead drop into my hands.

"Of course." She turns to give me a cheeky grin. "Right now, in fact."

My face pales. "What?"

"You heard me." Kasey cackles maniacally. "We're already dressed, so I'm taking you out!"

"What happened to moping in bed with a pint of cookie dough?"

"That's just something I told you so you wouldn't have time to argue." She waves me off. "You'll thank me later."

Somehow, I really, really doubt that.

My head pounds in time with the flashing club lights at The Blend. Not wanting to break back into the crowd just yet, I stand in the dark, uninhabited corner rounding to the bathrooms. My eyes wander around the crowded basement space, the urge to crawl into bed growing stronger by the second. Hanging my head, I lean my shoulder into the wall and sigh a deep breath of relief in the small oasis of isolation.

"Well, *hello,* beautiful," a voice slurs next to my ear.

Goose bumps prick my spine as his hot, repulsive breath makes contact with my skin. The urge to swing my elbow back into his crotch takes hold, but I manage to hold off for the time being.

Choosing peace, I act like I can't hear him—a perfectly reasonable response, considering the volume of the eardrum-bursting music thrumming around us. I jump as a calloused palm comes into contact with my forearm.

"Heyyyy," the same voice slurs. "Whasss your nameee?"

My chest grips with irritation as I swing around to face him. "None of your damn business. Now kindly take your dirty sausage mittens off me."

The man stares dumbly. I barely pass five-foot-six in the stilettos Kasey made me wear, and compared to me, he might as well be the Empire State Building.

I try to pry my arm away, but his grip holds strong. A surge of anger passes through me, taking all the space in my rib cage. *The nerve of this guy, I swear. Doesn't he know not to mess with women wearing pointy shoes?*

A warbled cry of agony tears out of the stranger's mouth as my stiletto smashes his shoe.

"Fugging bitsch!" he slurs, his eyes fuzzy with liquor and discomfort. Ignoring the damage to his foot, he lunges, his behemoth of a frame knocking me backward to the ground. My head cracks painfully against the concrete, sending stars shooting in front of my eyes.

The man's weight presses me into the floor as my lungs fight to take back the breath knocked out of me.

His breath is hot on my face and neck, reeking of cheap liquor and cigarette smoke. I choke down the bile rising in my throat as panic takes hold.

"Get *off* me!" I shout, a sound whisked away in the pounding of the heavy bass.

If the man hears me, he makes no inclination.

"You're hawwt," he blubbers, his face inching dangerously close to mine.

I manage to duck my head to the side, and his lips make contact with my cheek, sending a shudder of revulsion down my spine. I shove his chest, but the mass above me stays perfectly still. Claustrophobic dread makes my head fuzzy, and I begin thrashing wildly in his grip, my arms and legs flailing uselessly in the air.

Just when I start to think it's all over for me, the colossal hellion is ripped off. I suck in a much-needed breath as I sit upright, but the sight in front of me expels it just as quickly.

A massive, dark-haired man has his back turned to me. A fitted black suit covers his muscular frame, clinging deliciously to the taut muscles in his back and biceps as he pummels my attacker into the ground. I sit frozen in place for a moment, mesmerized by the power of his strikes.

After a second or two, my fight or flight kicks in, this time with wings. Scrambling to my feet, I take off toward the bar, scanning the room for a familiar face.

"Kasey!" I shout, my heart leaping with joy as I spot the top of her blond bob across the dance floor. Through sheer determination, I wriggle back through the tightly packed space, my stomach swirling with uneasiness with each wobbly step.

Kasey throws her head back in a laugh as a striking blond stranger whispers something into her ear, blissfully unaware of my mental freak-out.

As I near the pair, I debate my next move before I reach out and grip her forearm. Startled, she swings around to face me, her face relaxing when she realizes who it is.

"Cass, babe! I wondered where you went! I want you to meet—"

"Kase, I'm really sorry, but is there any way we can get out of here?" I shuffle my feet, unable to fully lift my eyes to meet hers.

Kasey's hazy eyes clear as she picks up on my uneasiness.

"What's the matter, hon? Did someone say something to you?" she questions, her voice hardening with that protectiveness I know and love.

"No, I'm fine! I mean..." Guilt swirls in my core at the thought of ruining her night with Green Eyes. He's sending me daggers over my best friend's shoulder, no doubt sensing his prospect for the night is about to be taken from him.

"You know me, girl. You say the word, and we're gone." She gives me a warm smile.

I return the favor, the fireworks in my belly beginning to fizzle. "As long as you're *sure* you don't mind."

She rolls her eyes. "Puh-lease. This place was starting to bore me anyway... No offense," she adds, turning to give Green Eyes a sheepish smile.

He huffs, sending me one last withering stare before stalking off to find other prey. Kasey grabs my forearm and begins parting the bodies, milling around the exit. Despite the chill crawling up my spine, I keep my eyes on the escape. I can't shake the feeling that a pair of dark, avenging eyes follows me the whole way out.

Chapter Two

I HAVEN'T HEARD A PEEP FROM CHAZ ALL DAY. I should be relieved, but I have to admit it's weird not being able to talk to someone you've spent the past year of your life with. Even if that someone turned out to be a giant bucket of turds.

My birth control alarm goes off, and I let out a bitter laugh as I turn it off. Little did Chaz know, I had almost come around to the idea of losing my virginity to him. I'd even started taking the pills in preparation, but I guess I won't be needing them anymore. What's the big deal with sex, anyways? I've gone almost twenty-two years without it, and I'm perfectly fine.

A little voice in the back of my head reminds me that "perfectly fine" people don't do what I have over the past few days, but I push it away. My mind wanders instead to the man from last night, the one who saved me. Why can't I date a man like that? One who will protect me at the first sign of trouble?

Actually, I'd take one who doesn't cheat on me at this point.

A small pang emanates from my chest, but I have little time to dwell on it as the door to my apartment bangs open. I don't bother looking up from my fetal position on the couch—the clacking of stilettos tells me all I need to know.

"Heyy! You ready to head out?" Kasey huffs as she takes in my pitiful state. "Dear Lord, Cass. How long have you been lying there?"

"I don't know. A while?" I shove my face further into the scratchy decorative pillow.

"Come on!" She rips the blanket from my shoulders. "Up and at 'em!"

I groan. "I don't know if I'm up for it. Having a bunch of sweaty, desperate men grinding on me all night sounds... unappealing."

"Well, lucky for you, we're not going to the club tonight."

I curl in on myself. "My sentiments apply to anything you have planned." I still haven't told her about what happened last night. The man who tried to attack me, the dread of knowing there was no way for me to protect myself. And then, my savior. The dark-haired stranger who appeared out of nowhere. *Who was he? Had he been watching me the whole night? How else did he know where I was?*

Kasey narrows her brilliant blues. "Nope. We're not doing this tonight. You're coming whether you like it or not. This funk you've been in isn't good for the soul," she declares, making a circle around me with her index finger. Glancing at a crusty bowl of what used to be ramen, she adds, "Or the eyes."

I give her a blank stare. "Need I remind you how long you seem to leave coffee cups in your car? *You,* of all people, shouldn't be complaining."

"We're not talking about that now." She waves me off. "We're talking about how you've been in a depressive hole for the last year. People are starting to worry, you know."

My brow shoots to my hairline. "By 'people', do you mean *you?*"

"Do you have some other best friend I don't know about? Of course it's me!"

I sigh. She has a point. I just can't seem to make myself care about anything. Not the state of my home, or my appearance, or even the fact I let a loser like Chaz string me along for a whole year.

I sigh. "Okay, *fine.* But I'm not doing my makeup," I assert, narrowing my eyes as her face breaks into a sly smile.

"Okay, okay, whatever you say, hun." She grins,

hoisting me off the couch by my forearm. "Just a *little* mascara and—"

I tune out the rest of her spiel, well aware that whatever I'm wearing tonight is utterly out of my hands.

———

When Kasey parks the car in front of a row of bland, boxy office buildings, I jerk the door open and tumble onto the pavement, having a sick urge to kiss the ground. *I've never been so happy to be out of a car in my life.*

"You good?" Kasey asks. "You look like you've just seen a ghost."

"Not seen." I keel over, placing my hands on my knees in an attempt to steady my breathing. "Just worried I was about to become one."

"Oh *God.*" Kasey rolls her eyes, clicking her key fob as she steps onto the sidewalk. "My driving isn't *that* bad."

I raise a brow. Thankfully, she has the decency to look slightly apologetic.

"So... where are we exactly?" I ask, taking in the row of plain concrete walled buildings.

"You'll figure it out soon. Come *on,* Cass!" she urges, waving a hand for me to follow.

I cross my arms, resisting the urge to huff and demand she explain herself. As we near the entrance, a pair of sliding glass doors whoosh open, greeting us with a smack of cool air as we pass inside. I rub my forearms as goose bumps crawl along my bare skin. If I'd had any inclination we'd be hanging out in some sterile office building tonight, I would have worn more than a tank top and cutoffs.

"Come on, slowpoke, I don't want them to start without us!" Kasey calls behind her, already at the top of the tall stairwell.

"What? *What* are they going to start without us?" I twist the gold chain around my thumb, my anxiety weighing me as I climb.

She gives me a bright, satisfied smile as I join her on the landing. "Our drawing class! Surprise!"

I cock my head. "What kind of art class happens at night?"

"The best kind."

I sigh, following her down another barren hallway with a begrudging pit growing in my stomach. I do *not* like surprises.

"Don't give me that look. You've gotta start living a little, Cass," she huffs.

Yeah, look how far that's gotten me. I used to love taking risks, loved the pounding of adrenaline flowing through my veins every time I did something spontaneous or dangerous. But it was those decisions that ruined my potential career as an artist. A pang of regret rips through my chest, as it so often did when I think of that stormy day on the water. My trusty surfboard, the brewing storm, the determination to ride just *one more* wave. Then, sickeningly, the memory of the riptide pulling me to the bottom of the reef, snapping my dominant hand in about twelve different places before dragging me back to the surface.

Phantom pain twinges in my left wrist, pulling me out of the memory as I unconsciously cradle it to my chest. It's good timing, too, because moments later, Kasey pauses in front of a door leading to one of the meeting rooms.

"Ready, Freddy?" She grins, pressing on the handle with barely contained excitement as she swings open the door.

Blinding, fluorescent light hits my eyes as we step inside, causing me to squint. A large, rounded podium sits in the center of the room, its entire circumference lined by at least thirty chairs and easels. All but two seats are filled, causing guilt to harden in my stomach. As much as I hate surprises, I hate being late that much more.

I'm torn from my anxiety-fueled trance as a voice sounds to my left.

"Welcome! I was worried we would have to start

without you two." With her paint-stained apron and tired, sunken eyes, it's obvious she's the instructor. Her emerald eyes shine with kindness underneath messy, unkempt brows as she addresses us. "We're just about to bring out your subject, so if you guys want to grab your seats, we'll get started right away!"

"I'm so sorry about that. I tried to get us here as fast as I could, I swear," Kasey apologizes, smiling meekly at the woman. I mirror her, then follow Kasey over to the two empty seats. As I look around the room, I'm struck by how skewed the gender ratio is. There's always a healthy distribution of both in all the art classes I've attended. But here... it's *all women*.

"All right, everyone, I know you've all been waiting *very* patiently," the instructor's teasing lilt fills the space, sending several students into a fit of giggles. "Without further ado, I give you... *your subject.*"

Gasps litter the room as soon as she utters the words. I crane my head around my easel, trying to see what all the fuss is about, but the podium remains empty. My gaze swings to Kasey and her strange look of hungry anticipation.

"Kase... we're not going to be drawing some sort of wild animal, are we?" I ask, my chest tightening in fear as I imagine a giant Bengal tiger being led onto the stage and promptly mauling my face.

Kasey ignores my question, stifling a giggle with

her hand as her eyes lock onto something to the left of her canvas. Having more than my share of suspense, I jump from my seat, pressing on my tiptoes to peer over the top of my canvas.

And *that's* when I get an eyeful of some man's bare ass.

Chapter Three

I PLOP BACK INTO MY SEAT AND TURN TO MY—
supposedly—best friend, my face a picture of mortification.

"Why didn't you tell me this was a *nude* painting
class?" I hiss, sweat starting to pool beneath my thin
cotton tank.

Kasey shrugs, never taking her eyes off the spectacle in front of us. The very masculine, very *naked*
spectacle.

My chest squeezes. I'm not naïve. Sure, I haven't
technically had sex, but I've seen more than my fair
share of portraits and sculptures of the male form. So
why is the thought of having to detail every inch of his
manhood turning me into a timid, nervous wreck?

"Are you gonna pick up that pencil and start, or
just stare off into space like a weirdo?"

Kasey's teasing lilt brings me back to the cold, harsh reality. My eyes scan the room as I twist my necklace around my thumb, realizing with a jolt that every other person has already started drawing.

Shakily, I pick up one of the charcoal pencils laid out at my station. I attempt to raise my eyes from my barren canvas, but fail miserably. As if knowing my inner turmoil, Kasey snickers beside me.

Come on, Cass. Why are you making this so weird? He's probably getting off on all these people looking at him.

"Everything all right, dear?"

I jump at the quiet voice next to my ear. My heart thrums wildly as I turn to meet the kind green eyes of the instructor.

"Yeah. I'm having a hard time deciding where I want to start, I guess," I mumble, wanting so badly for her to stop staring at me with that inquisitive gaze.

"Oh God, *I know, right?* So many great areas to start." Her lids lower with a faraway expression that tells me she knows *exactly* where she would start. She shakes her head, returning to reality and plastering another pleasant smile onto her face.

"How about another angle? Sometimes that really helps me when I'm undecided!"

Before I have a chance to respond, she turns her attention to the model.

"Hon! Would you mind turning this way a little? I don't think this young lady has a good enough view."

I open my mouth to insist something like *no, that's really not necessary,* but the instructor has moved on to another victim before I have time to blink.

When I turn back to my canvas, I can't help but to let a little gasp escape from my mouth. Standing directly in front of me—in the *nude,* mind you—is the epitome of a Greek god. I can't bring myself to look directly at his face, but it's impossible to take my eyes from the rest of his exposed body. Standing well over six feet tall, every inch of his frame is taut with the muscles of a bodybuilder. His well-defined abs glisten under the bright lights and have a trail to a perfect V between his hips. What's below that—thankfully—is covered by the top of my canvas. Given the rest of his stature, I have a sneaking suspicion that even *that* organ is impressive.

I lick my lips subconsciously, my mind turning to a situation involving me, the mystery model, a bottle of tequila, and all the wondrous things he could do to me. My neck warms at the thought. *Jesus, what is* wrong *with me? I've gone from prude to sexual deviant in less than two minutes.*

Shaking my head to clear away any impure thoughts, I bring the pencil to canvas once more. The tip hovers just above the frame as I'm caught in a furious debate with myself whether I have the nerve to go lower.

Or higher, for that matter. I can't seem to look at his face any easier than his *junk,* for God's sake. With a huff, I begin sketching the outline of his chest, my wrist twinging slightly with every minuscule movement. A pit of sadness hardens in my gut as I am reminded, once more, of the consequences of my decisions. If I had just listened to my brother and hadn't been trying to ride some crazy adrenaline-fueled high, maybe—just *maybe*—I could have had the art career I'd always dreamed of.

I pause as I begin to outline his fists, noticing for the very first time how bruised and cracked the skin is between his knuckles. Like he's been hitting something. Or *someone.*

I swallow nervously at the thought, my hand freezing above my canvas with the understanding of the damage he could do if he wanted to.

"Holy shit, dude. That looks awesome."

I'm pulled out of my anxiety-ridden bubble as Kasey speaks out, her eyes wide in awe as she stares at the swill I managed to get onto the canvas.

"Thanks. It's really not, though... I mean, compared to what I used to be able to do..." A wave of exhaustion overcomes me as I speak.

"Oh please, stop being so wishy-washy! It looks so

cool and realistic. The only thing you're missing is his head and... you know. His *head*." She wiggles her brows with a wicked grin.

"It just feels so...wrong. I can't objectify him like that." I lower my voice to a hush, praying the man standing not two feet from me is somehow hard of hearing.

Kasey rolls her eyes. "Puh-lease. Look around you, hon. Not one single woman in here isn't eye fucking that absolute piece of man candy."

I raise a brow. "Eye candy? Really?"

She huffs. "Yes, really! What do you think he's here for, huh? You really think a man *that* hot isn't gonna profit off that shit?"

"You make it all sound so wholesome," I deadpan. "And here I thought this was all about the art."

"Art shmart." Kasey wrinkles her nose. "The only thing the ladies in this class care about is sex appeal. As it should be, in my humble opinion."

I swear a low chuckle rumbles from the stranger's chest, but I don't have the nerve to look away from Kasey's face to see if I'm right. Rolling my eyes, I turn back to my canvas, fire running across my skin as if a certain model is watching me.

The soles of ballet flats slap against the floor, drawing nearer and filling me with a sense of dread. She isn't *my* teacher, per se, but ever since attending one of the most prestigious art colleges in the country, I've come to think of every authority figure in the art community as my judge. The last thing I want is to disappoint her with the sad sight of my scribbles.

"Oh my..." A soft, reverent tone sounds directly behind my right shoulder. "This is... *lovely*. You managed to get so much movement and life in this small section of anatomy," she mutters, brushing her finger against the dark smudges of charcoal.

"Uh... thank you so much." My cheeks warm the longer she stays frozen, drinking in the sketch with hungry eyes.

"What's your name?" she asks, never looking away from the canvas.

"Cass. Well, Cassandra, technically. But I really do prefer Cass, if you don't mind." Thankfully, the poor woman is still too engrossed with the art to pay my rambling any attention.

"Cass... how many art classes have you taken before tonight?"

I shift in my seat. "Plenty. Well, not for the past year, but I actually attended art school for a while."

"Pardon me for questioning." She straightens with a thrilled glint in her eye. "It's just... Well, to be frank with you, I haven't seen this caliber of work in quite some time. And I'm not as young as I seem." She winks. "I would love to see some of your other pieces if you have time in the next week or so." She rubs her palms together excitedly. "Any of your old pieces from school would do. It doesn't need to be a brand-new composition, *naturally*." She throws her head back as if sharing an inside joke with me.

I smile politely, not having the heart to tell her that all of my old art has met the same fate: death by bonfire. The same day I learned that I would never gain full mobility of my hand, *naturally*.

I'm saved from the obligation to respond as a woman on the other side of the circle raises her hand for assistance. With what, I can't fathom. I'm just thankful for the distraction.

The instructor gives me an apologetic smile as she walks over to her, calling back over her shoulder with a promise, "I'll grab you to talk after class!"

I let out a breath I didn't know I'd been holding in, returning to the sad little scribbles that garnered me so much attention. My chest swells with pride for the first time in over a year—even though I know in my heart that it's undeserved.

"Cass? Helloooo, earth to Cass!"

I snap my head, nearly knocking heads with Kasey.

"Jeez! Why the hell are you so close?"

Her eyes narrow. "*Babes,* I've been calling you for the past minute. You've just been in your own little bubble. Class is over."

I snap my eyes around the room. Sure enough, most of the ladies have collected their canvases and begun milling around the room, their eyes searching and hungry. Moments later, the male model reappears with a thin white towel around his waist, his hair tousled like he's been running his hands through it. Feeling an urge to run my tongue along the bare skin, I rip my eyes from him in mortification. *What on earth is happening to me? I was never this perverse with Chaz.*

Before I have the chance to spiral at the thought of my cheating ex, Kasey tugs at my arm, voicing something excitable into my ear.

"What? I missed all of that, sorry," I say, purposely ignoring the irritated scowl she gives me. Rolling her eyes, she grips my chin in her hand and forces it back in the direction I just turned from.

Mr. Model is walking toward us. No, not walking —*stalking,* with the purpose of a ravenous animal who has just spotted dinner. From the way Kasey elbows me, I have no doubt she's trying to draw my attention to the tent he's pitching. My eyes shoot to his face, not having the courage to look below his waist.

With a strong, stubbled jaw and piercing dark-brown eyes set above full lips and a slightly crooked nose, his handsomeness quite literally takes my breath away. This man belongs in the newest Marvel movie, strolling a red carpet with a supermodel on his arm. So what the hell is he doing here in this sleepy little beach town?

My face must give away the power he has over me because a smirk carves its way onto his handsome face. It's a familiar smile, one I swear has made its way into my dreams before.

But that can't be. I've never seen this man in my life—I'm sure of it. I wouldn't forget a face like that. As he nears, I take in his entire frame slowly, realization dawning on me like a bucket of ice-cold water.

I know this man. I know him well.

His eyes dart to my neckline, taking in the sun charm lying between my cleavage.

"You're still wearing that old thing, huh?"

My chest constricts. *The necklace. He's talking about the necklace he gave me.*

"Jace! You're naked!"

I curse myself, fighting the urge to clap my hand over my mouth. *After all this time, after he looks like THAT, and that's what you come up with? Way to go, brain...*

Jace looks like he's holding back a laugh. "This is a nude drawing class. I kind of have to be."

"I realize that." I take a breath, really wishing I'd taken yoga so I could practice the whole foot-in-mouth thing right now. "Is this, you know... what you do for a living now?"

God, can I be any more cringy? Dear earth, if you want to swallow me up, now is the time.

This time, he does laugh, throwing his head back and letting out a low, husky sound. The allure of it catches me off guard, and I kind of just stand there gaping at him like a goldfish for a few seconds. *Dear God, are those DIMPLES? How have I never noticed those before...*

"No, not at all." His dark eyes shine. "The proceeds from this class go to a charity I'm working with. The real model got sick, so they asked me to step in."

And thank God they did.

The thought enters my mind so powerfully that it knocks the breath from my lungs. Jace doubles over in laughter, and it's only then that I realize I said it out loud.

Before Jace has a chance to say something like, "I'd like you to get away from me now, weirdo," one of the class members saunters over and taps him on the shoulder. With her perfectly done-up face and six-inch cherry-red heels, I recognize her immediately. She and her friend were part of the group doing the most shameless ogling, much more interested in looking than getting anything of substance on paper.

Her tongue darts out, wetting her lips as she runs a painted fingernail down his exposed chest while whispering something unintelligible into his ear. Without taking his dark eyes off me, he grabs the hand, yanks it back down by the woman's side, then drops her wrist as if she's contagious.

With a tight smile, he turns to her, speaking just low enough so I can't make out a damn thing being said. Whatever it is, though, morphs the woman's expression into one of extreme embarrassment. She shoots me a look I can't quite make out before skittering back to her group of friends, mouthing an apology over her shoulder.

The image of her brushing his bare chest swirls in my mind, sending a surge of white-hot rage through my veins. I give myself a little shake, trying to get my traitorous hormones under control as two more women take the place of Red Heels.

This is *Jace,* for fuck's sake. He's my best friend, the one who taught me how to surf and showed me the best shells to collect along the shoreline. The one who protected me and held me together whenever I scraped my knee or had my heart broken.

The one I left behind four years ago, and the friendship I missed most when my accident happened. Seeing him here now, looking so different, the pain comes back tenfold.

My wrist twinges, dragging me back to the present and the unsettling sight of Jace locked in conversation with the two blondes from earlier. Suddenly, all my clothes feel unbearably tight against my skin, stretching and pulling uncomfortably against the rising heat in my chest.

The overwhelming urge to stomp over and crack their two perfectly botoxed heads together pours over me in waves. *I need to get the hell out of here.*

I scan the room for a familiar blond bob and notice her at the far corner of the room, deeply entrenched in a hushed conversation with the instructor. I make my way to them, a pang of jealousy ringing in my chest at the visual reminder of Kasey's ability to charm the pants off anyone she comes into contact with.

She looks up as I near, and her eyes light with excitement. "Cass, babe! We were *just* talking about you."

"Well, that's rarely a good thing."

Kasey rolls her eyes. "*Actually,* we were talking about how kick-ass your sketch is. So ha!"

My cheeks warm. I have a hard enough time accepting compliments for things I feel *good* about, let alone for things I know I don't deserve. The instructor stares with those damn perceptive eyes of hers, so I have to respond no matter how it makes me feel.

"That's very kind of you," I say, stretching my lips over my teeth in what I hope is a smile. "I'm sure there were plenty of nice pieces in the room tonight."

For a moment, the woman drops her neutral expression and flinches, her nose scrunched like she just discovered a particularly nasty pile of dog shit on the floor.

"Oh, honey, *no,*" she says in a hushed whisper, her eyes going wide. "If you knew how many penis drawings I have had to critique over the years... well, that's a story for some other time." She lets out a small shudder. "The point is, I know real talent when I see it. You've got *more* than enough of it, Cass. I'm interested to see what you can do with other mediums."

Looking into her kind, hazel eyes, I want nothing more than to reach into my chest and yank out my aching heart. Tears threaten to make their way into my eyes, but I push all of the emotion aside before it chokes me. I can't break down. Not here. Not like this. Not in front of this kind woman trying to pay me a compliment. It's not her fault that even after all this time, the scars from learning I'd never create again are just as painful as the day I donned them.

Before I have the chance to respond, the woman's attention is called to someone over my shoulder. Whatever higher power is up there must have heard my pleading.

"Here, take my card. Text the number on the back, and we'll be in touch, okay?" she asks, not even bothering to wait for my response before shoving the square into my hand and rushing off.

"Yeah, right. We'll be in touch," I mumble, my shoulders slumping as I shove the card into my back pocket to be forgotten about. Kasey's eyes search my face, but I don't have the strength to face her. Apart from my brother, she's the only one who really knows what happened and how it affected me. Coincidently, they were also the only ones who didn't treat me like a leper when things got particularly dark.

"Cass? Where did you go?"

Kasey's voice, soft and full of concern, pulls me out of my impending spiral. I raise my eyes to meet her and give her a small smile to let her know I'm okay.

Because I *am* okay. I have to be, after all.

"Let's just get out of here, okay?" I ask, hoping she doesn't hear the desperation tangling in my words.

Without hesitating a beat, she nods in the affirmative, taking my hand in hers to lead me and my wobbling knees out of the room. I leave my sad excuse of a drawing where it lay on my easel, the sketchy scribbles and jagged edges taunting me all the way out.

Or maybe it's that same pair of dangerously dark eyes following me home to make their way into my dreams tonight.

Chapter Four

BRRRRRING... BRRRRRRING... BRRRRRING

"Oh for the love of—" I grumble incoherently as I throw my arm in the direction of my phone. "Who in their right mind would call someone at this early hour of... Oh..." I check the clock on my lock screen. 12:30.

I groan and flop back onto the pillow as I thumb the green button to accept the call, not even bothering to check who it is.

"Morning, sleeping beauty. How's the hangover?"

The smirk palpable in Kasey's voice makes me want to reach through the phone and strangle her. The woman's damn cheetah-like metabolism makes sure she never has anything worse than a mild headache the morning after, and her favorite thing to do is rub it in the face of poor, sick saps like me. My head is—*indeed*—pounding after that third bottle of Pinot we polished off after the class, and I'm in no state to pretend otherwise.

"Bad enough to make me decide I'll never drink again," I grumble as I blindly feel on the dresser for the bottle of aspirin I keep there. "It feels like a thousand tiny men are sledgehammering my head from the inside out if that gives you any idea."

"I appreciate the detail. Anything I can do for you?"

"You can put me out of my misery," I groan, dramatically throwing my arm over my eyes to block out some of the blinding light streaming through my curtains.

She huffs, and I grin, imagining her rolling her eyes.

"Did you take anything for the pain?"

"That was the first thing I did... right after cursing the gods for making me wake another day in this cruel, cruel world."

"You're such a drama queen." I can practically *feel* her rolling her eyes. "Serves you right for drinking your emotions away."

"I'm pretty sure you were the one who came up with that idea."

"Exactly. No one should ever listen to me. I'm a wreck, Cass."

A full-bellied laugh pours from my mouth, causing

me to wince. "Dammit. Don't make me laugh, you sadist."

"You know, you wouldn't have such a bad hangover if you sweated it out in pilates like I did this morning."

"I'm sorry, did I say you were a sadist? I meant masochist."

Kasey sucks her teeth. "Point taken. At least drink some water or take a shower. You've got work later, right?"

I groan, pulling my phone from my ear to check. "I hate how you know my schedule better than I do."

"Someone has to. Have you thought any more about what happened last night? With Jace? He seemed pretty upset when we left."

"Oh God, not this again." I palm my forehead, willing the images of his naked torso to leave my mind. "We went over this last night. He probably hates me, and I wouldn't blame him."

"He doesn't *hate you.*"

"Oh yeah?" I huff. "I hate *myself* for how I left. The last words we spoke to each other were... friendship ending. He probably wants nothing to do with me."

"That's really not what it seemed like last night."

I sigh, my shoulders slumping. I don't expect her to understand it. The relationship Jace and I had growing up... was so much deeper than friendship. We were each other's soulmates, just without the romantic parts. There was no Cass without Jace, no yin without yang. Now... now there's nothing. So much time has passed, and we're basically strangers. And the worst part is, it's all my fault.

"I think I'm going to take that shower now," I mumble. "Miranda is working with me today, and if I'm late, she'll tear me a new one."

"Okay, babes. You know where I am if you need me," Kasey says, her tone filled with concern.

"Always. Love you."

"Love you. Have a good time at work! Oh, and give Miranda a middle finger salute from me."

I chuckle. If anyone hates my manager more than me, it's Kasey. I let out a heavy sigh as the screen goes black, dreading the long day ahead of me as I trudge into the bathroom.

I turn the water as hot as it will go, then step under the stream. The heat numbs my skin, lulling me into a dream-like state as I stand under the torrent of steaming water. My mind wanders, reels, and flips, running through endless scenarios and torturous memories. Then, suddenly, I'm not in the shower anymore. I'm somewhere else, reliving the memory of that horrible day four years ago...

Rain drums against my umbrella, the scent of wet

dirt assaulting my senses and twisting my stomach with nausea.

I squeeze Jace's hand, unable to take my eyes off the coffin being lowered into the hole in the earth. What do you even say when your best friend's father is being put into the ground? Words like 'sorry' won't cut it, but my brain is incapable of coming up with anything else.

But I have to think of something soon. My plane leaves in an hour, and I haven't even told him I'm going.

"I'm so sorry, Jace," I whisper, my chest constricting at how hollow the words sound. "I wish there was something I could do."

His fingers squeeze mine, and he tilts his head to give me a sad little smile. "I know. I'm just lucky to have you here. I honestly couldn't get through today without having you by my side."

It feels like a knife is pushed in my heart. God, I can't tell him now. Any other time but now. I should have told him weeks ago when I found out I got accepted, but his dad was sick, and it was just never a good time. Now...

My alarm goes off, letting me know I have half an hour before I need to leave for the airport. God, this will crush him.

I'm able to keep it to myself until the crowd starts

mingling toward their cars, but when Jace starts leading me toward his, I dig my heels into the earth.

"What's wrong? Did you drop something?" Jace looks behind me, already beginning to scour the ground.

"Jace, stop." I grip his arm, and he turns to face me. "I... can't go back to the house with everyone."

"What are you talking about?"

"I... I have a plane to catch," I whisper, watching as a series of emotions run across his face. "I got into that school in Paris. I wanted to tell you sooner, but—"

"But you thought my father's funeral would be the best time." He takes a step back, and the look in his eyes makes me wish the ground would swallow me whole. "Really, Cass? You're leaving now, *of all times? A little heads-up would have been nice, but I guess you only reserve that for people you care about."*

"Jace, I do *care about you! You're my best friend for crying—"*

"Best friends don't abandon each other when they're trying to bury their fathers!" he bellows, causing a few of his family members to glance our way. "You know what? Just get the fuck out of here. Go to your fancy school and forget about this place. Forget about me." *He looks me up and down, his lip curled with malice. "I doubt it'll be hard for you."*

My heart lodges in my throat as he turns away, and I sprint to catch up. "Jace, stop! You know I care about you! I wanted to tell you sooner, but there just wasn't any time! It wasn't a good time!" I bawl, gripping onto his arm and attempting to get him to face me. "I'm sorry."

"Sorry doesn't cut it, does it?" He turns his head just enough for me to catch the bitter smile straining his lips. "Leave. There's nothing we can say to each other that won't permanently damage us, and you have a plane to catch."

When I don't move, Jace narrows his beautiful chocolate eyes. They're full of malice, but something else swims in his gaze. Something like regret.

"I said leave! Don't you realize you're not fucking wanted here? Go!" he chokes out, sounding close to tears. Before I have time to respond, he jumps into his car, slamming the door to drown out my sobs. I don't know if he looks back, but I can't take my eyes from his taillights as he speeds down the road away from me. Away from us.

God, what have I done?

I gasp, my eyes flinging open as the water turns frigid. *Damn, how long have I been out for?* I turn the shower off and rest my forehead against the tile, my shoulders drooping with a heavy sigh. My water bill this month will probably be astronomical.

The pit from earlier hardens my stomach as I reflect on the day our friendship ended. Before, I thought Jace and I were unbreakable. He was the sun to my shadow, the yin to my yang. And then, one day, he just... wasn't. When he didn't reach out after a few days of me being in Paris, I assumed he needed more time to cool off. Those days stretched into weeks, then months, and it became clear he was probably happier without me. I never tried to reach out or mend what I had broken.

A piece of me has always been missing since Jace and I stopped talking, though I never realized just how big until yesterday. After seeing him now that all this time has passed, I'm filled with enough regret to drown in.

I shake the feeling away, knowing I need to focus on getting ready for work before I end up late and fired. I step out of the shower with a sense of dread for the coming day. I can't imagine it will be productive, considering I can't stop thinking about a certain muscley, devastatingly handsome man.

"Do you want any sugar in that?"

The middle-aged man across the counter doesn't even bother looking up from his smartphone as he gives me a gruff, "Hmph!"

I hold in an exasperated sigh. Working in this coffee shop has taken a toll on my view of humanity. If I had a nickel for every asshole I had to serve with a sickly sweet smile, I'd buy an island so I'd never have to come in contact with a single shitty soul again.

I rattle off his total, and he shoves a debit card into the reader without ever looking up, then turns and steps over to the pickup area while I busy myself over the espresso machine.

Over the sounds of brewing coffee, the front doorbell rings out, alerting me to the entrance of another customer.

"I'll be with you in a sec!" I call out, experience telling me I have exactly five seconds to take their order before a hissy fit ensues.

"Take your time, please."

At the words, I freeze, every muscle in my body tightening as the familiar husk washes over me.

"Jace," I breathe, my eyes widening in shock as I take in his handsome smile. He's dressed in a simple black button-down and slacks, but his air of charisma still makes him look out of place in the dingy little coffee shop. My eyes trail over his frame hungrily, seized by the desire to find out what's beneath his belt.

"Like what you see?"

My body jerks, his voice like a bucket of ice-cold water dragging me back to reality.

Not wanting him to know the effect he has on me,

I roll my eyes. "I'm glad to see your ego is just as large after all this time."

He throws back his head in a loud, throaty chuckle. The sound makes my knees wobble, and I'm suddenly grateful for the stability of the counter between us.

"And you haven't lost an ounce of that sass. Good to know." He smirks, gazing at me with those piercing black eyes of his.

"It just gets worse by the day, I'm afraid." My heart does a little somersault as his dimple makes a grand appearance.

Jace opens his mouth to speak, but before he gets the chance, Mr. Baldy from earlier clears his throat.

"Now listen here, hussy," he snaps, his double chin wobbling with anger. "I'm trying to be nice, but I've been waiting here patiently while you two had your little flirt fest. Now I either want my fucking cup of coffee or I want my money back. What's it going to be?"

My chest clenches at the venom in his words. I want nothing more than to reel around and throw the scalding bean water onto his pompous, fat face. But more than that, I really don't want to lose my job.

One look at Jace tells me if anyone is going to throw coffee in somebody's face, it'll be him.

"What the fuck did you just call her?" Jace's voice

is deadly quiet, and a shiver runs down my spine. I've never seen that expression on his face before, and it makes me scared for the person it's aimed at.

The man's face purples. "I'm not talking to you, asshole. Get lost."

Jace quirks a brow. "There's no need to be so rude."

"Like I said, get fucking lost."

Jace's eyes light with fury as he lunges toward the man, grabbing him by the front of his sweat-stained shirt. I'm afraid Jace will hit him, but instead, he uses the leverage to whisper something in the man's ear. The blood drains from his face, and he stumbles backward as Jace releases his grip.

"Have a nice day," Jace coos, waggling his fingers as the man all but sprints from the store. "Fucking prick."

I stand frozen, my mouth agape as I try to process what just happened.

"What the hell did you say to that guy?"

"Nothing I didn't mean." His eyes darken with the reminder. "I'm sorry about that... I just couldn't stand there and let him talk to you that way." He sighs, running a hand through his tousled black hair. "Nobody treats anyone like a *person* anymore. Especially those working in the service industry. The shit you have to go through on a daily basis...my hat goes off to you."

My lips twitch upward. "You're not wearing a hat, though."

Jace narrows his eyes, the effect dulled by the smile tugging at his lips. "It was a metaphor, but thank you for the clarification."

"It's my pleasure."

We stay locked in a staring contest of wits, neither willing to break the tension dangling in the space between us. Jace goes first, letting his eyes drag across my chest, busting at the seams of my ill-fitting polyester work shirt.

Fire warms my skin where his eyes travel, and I clear my throat to relieve some of the sexual energy swirling between us.

"So, um... can I get you anything? I mean, this is a coffee shop after all..."

My words falter at the look in his eyes. I can't quite make it out, but whatever it is seems... dark. Hungry, even.

"I think I know exactly what I want. And it's not coffee," he murmurs, his voice so low I barely catch it.

"Excuse me?"

"What are you doing tonight?" he asks, ignoring my question.

"Nothing, I guess? We close at five, and I usually

just rush home to get my bra off and hop into bed with a book."

As the words tumble out, I have to stifle a groan. Maybe I *was* dropped on my head as an infant like my brother says.

I'm not brave enough to look him in the eye, but if I have to guess, the man is sporting one of his infamous grins. For some reason, the thought makes my heart clench.

"Perfect. I'll pick you up at seven, then. It's a bit of a... fancier place, so any sort of formal dress would be fine."

It appears my last two brain cells have left the building because I stand there gaping for several seconds, my brain unable to comprehend what he's telling me.

"I'm sorry... are you asking me on a date?"

"No. I'm *telling* you I will be picking you up for our date at seven. Tonight. Your place." He pauses at the look on my face, his grin growing wider. "Unless of course you'd rather spend another riveting night braless in bed. Because I could arrange that too, you know."

He says the last part with a wink, and my cheeks flush, the thought of the two of us half naked and rolling around in my tiny bed too much for my heart to take.

His eyes darken at my stunned silence, creeping lustfully over my frame. "Oh, so you *do* want the latter option. Interesting." He grins playfully, lowering his voice to a deep husk and stepping closer to the counter. "I personally think you'll like the outcome."

My heart is trying to beat its way out of my chest, but I swallow hard and steel my gaze.

"And what makes you think that?" I huff, crossing my arms over my chest.

Bad move. The question supposed to demoralize him only seems to be stoking the fire.

"Wouldn't you like to know?" he asks, eyes darkening to a pitch black as his tongue darts out, wetting his lower lip.

God, I bet that tongue would feel amazing on my— wait! No! Bad Cass!

Chills run down my spine as he continues to glower, no doubt running through a thousand delicious scenarios like the one I just shoved from my mind.

What are you even planning to do? Fuck him over the counter? As if all the bleach in the world would be enough to get rid of the mess we'd make.

My core throbs at the mere thought of it, and I know I need to get him out of here before my resolve weakens, and I really *do* fuck him over this very counter. The ravenous look in his eyes told me he wouldn't object to the idea, that's for damn sure.

"So, uh... seven, you say?" I squeak, hating the way my voice cracks.

"Seven." His eyes flash with some indiscernible emotion before he pushes off the counter, discreetly tugging at the material by his crotch.

I stifle a smile. *Now* I know what that look was for.

"I'll see you then."

"Yes. You will."

With that, he turns on his heels and stalks out the way he came in—with the confidence of a man who knows he's about to get *exactly* what he wants.

Guess I'll have to start taking my birth control again.

Chapter Five

"No... no... no... no... ughhhh. No!"

I groan in dismay as the entire contents of my closet lie on the ground in various discarded heaps. It's over before it even began. I have *nothing* to wear.

I fist the black miniskirt that had been a gift from Kasey before I left for college and hold it up to the light. A year ago, the thing might have just barely reached the bottom of my ass. Now, I doubt it'll make it over one of my thighs.

A curse spews from my lips as I toss the detestable piece of cloth across the room to join its fallen brethren. Not for the first time, I wish the ample hour-glass frame I inherited from my mom could be traded for the slim frame and height my best friend has been blessed with. At least then, I might be able to shop for clothes that fit me.

Lost deeply to my woes, I barely hear my front door slam open. *Speak of the devil and she shall appear...*

"Never fear, your best friend is here!" Kasey calls out, slamming the door behind her before her footsteps sound toward the bedroom. "I got your text that you were having a hard time picking an outfi—oh, for fuck's sake! You didn't tell me you set off a bomb in here!"

"Har har, very funny," I mumble into my hands. "I've literally tried on every single piece of clothing— well, the ones that would fit me—and *nothing*. I. Have. Nothing. To. Wear."

"Geez, no need to sound so morbid." Kasey huffs, carefully treading through the sea of clothing toward me. "He would probably prefer if you showed up in the nude anyway. Just saying."

"Oh my God, you're *so* not making this better," I groan, raising my head to look at the bounty of dresses she's holding in her arms. "What are those?"

"*These,* my sweet, sweet friend, are your ticket to some dick tonight." A devious smile lights her face. "You are gonna look so hot, he'll be coming in his pants when he sees you. I guarantee it."

"Ah, yes, cum-soaked pants. What every woman dreams of. Truly."

She narrows her eyes, obviously not appreciating

my sarcastic tone. "I could do without the attitude, you know. Since I rushed over here to help you and all."

I open my mouth to remind her that in no way, shape, or form did I actually *ask* her to come over, but the indignant look on her face stops me.

"You're right." I sigh. "I'm sorry for being a bit of a bitch. It's just that I'm nervous. I haven't been on a date since... well, since before Chaz, that's for sure."

Kasey wrinkles her nose at the mention of my ex and the lack of actual dates he had taken me on during the year we were together. A little ironic, considering he was going to cheat on me by taking some *other girl* out to a romantic dinner.

The memory puts a sour taste in my mouth, so I push the thoughts from my mind and focus on the real problem at hand—my lack of wardrobe options.

Kasey pushes a slinky, strappy red dress into my arms and thrusts her pointer finger in the direction of the bathroom.

"Go," she orders, narrowing her eyes in preparation for my disagreement. "And don't you dare give me the whole *it's too small* spiel. I know you have this warped idea in your head that you look like a hippo in tight dresses. So just do us both a huge favor, and *trust me.* You're gonna look hot."

Not having the energy to argue with her, I

begrudgingly let her place the leg warmer into my hands and stomp over to the bathroom to change.

After stripping my clothes, I pause, staring at the tiny strip of fabric in my hands as I say a tiny prayer to the dress gods.

Dear God or Goddess... Whoever you are up there... please allow me to get into this chinese finger trap without injury. And more importantly, give me the strength to get out. *Keep my will strong and the seams of this dress stronger. Amen.*

Taking in one last steeling breath, I shove the dress's bodice over my head and shoulders, slinking my arms through the tiny circumference like a double-jointed snake.

Okay, halfway there. Now for the hard part.

With the dress now snugly wound around my throat and cutting off my airflow, I reach the hem and attempt to yank it past my full D cups, panic slowly creeping in as the fabric barely budges.

"Kasey!" I yell, my panic palpable. "I need your help!"

A second later, she bursts through the door, her eyes wild and searching for potential threats. "What? What is it?"

"I'm stuck."

Her face drops, unamused as she takes in the situation.

"I can see that. I thought something terrible happened with the way you were screaming."

"Something terrible *did* happen!" I screech, my arms still stuck by my ears as the fabric continues to strangle the air from my lungs.

Kasey sighs and steps over to me. "There's no need to be so dramatic about it. I guess I should have warned you that this dress is a little tricky to get into."

"You think?"

Her eyes flash with irritation. "Watch it, or I'll just leave you like this. Lord only knows how long it would take you to get out of that thing if I wasn't here."

Stupid Chinese finger trap. Whichever man's bright idea it was to make women's clothes this hard to get into needs to be shot.

"Can you *please* just help me get this thing off? I'll give you a million dollars," I plead, letting loose the full weight of my puppy dog eyes on her. Which probably looked a little ridiculous, considering I currently look like one of those birds with their necks stuck in the little plastic rings they use for twelve packs.

"I can help you get it *on*. Your boy toy will have to do the other part for you." She grins, reaching to the hem to help wiggle it past my breasts.

Either out of practice or sheer willpower, Kasey manages to get it all the way down. I stand there like a stuffed sausage, not quite brave enough to look in the mirror and realize how ridiculous I look.

"Oh my God." Kasey's eyes are wide as she gives me a slow once-over. "It's even better than I could have imagined. You look *smoking,* girl."

I give her a dubious look that screams, "*Yeah, right.*" Kasey huffs, planting a hand on her hip as she grabs my arm to spin me toward the mirror.

And might I just say—*holy shit.* She's right. I stare at my reflection open-mouthed, sliding my palms lightly over the sleek red fabric that hugs every curve of my body and gives me that gorgeous, hourglass silhouette. I turn slightly to the side, marveling how the dress accentuates my already full breasts and hips.

"Kasey... it's beautiful," I breathe, not wanting to look away from the mirror just yet.

She grins as I continue checking myself out like the egotistical maniac. "It's yours now."

I freeze, catching her eye in the mirror to give her a look of suspicion.

"What?" She shrugs. "It looks like shit on me. It needs someone with curves to fill it out and, well... we both know I'm hella lacking in that department."

I roll my eyes as she tugs unhappily at the crop top covering her chest. "Kase, everyone and their mom would kill for your figure. You look like a model, for God's sake."

She crinkles her nose. "Says *you*, the girl who's practically the dark-haired Marilyn Monroe. Do you know what I would give for an ass that doesn't hurt to sit on?"

I can't help but giggle.

Just then, a knock on the front door sounds. My head whips over to face Kasey as a tsunami of nerves roils in my stomach.

"I think your loverboy is hereee," she coos. "Should I let him in?"

The first thought that comes to mind is *hell no*. The last thing I want is for my date to be interrogated by my best friend, but I'm not exactly ready, either.

"Fine," I groan, shooting her a look of warning. "But you have to promise to be *nice* to him. No snide remarks, no threats of chopping off his manhood if he hurts me. Okay?"

For a moment, she looks like she wants to disagree, but nods.

"Fine. I'll be nice. But if he *does* hurt you, I *will* chop off his most prized possession. You can be the one to make sure he knows that."

With a wink and a wave, she exits the bathroom. I brace my palms against the sink and let out a breath I didn't know I've been holding in. What I wouldn't give for a shot of something strong right now...

The faint sounds of muffled conversation make

their way to my ears, pulling me out of my anxiety-filled musings and screaming for me to get a move on. Knowing I have roughly five minutes before Kasey scars the beautiful man in my living room, I whip some mascara onto my lashes and finish the look off with a light touch of blush over my cheekbones.

Relieved I finally pass for someone who gets a full eight hours of sleep a night, I turn on my heel and make my way out into the living room.

"There she is!"

I grin at Kasey's animated greeting, and before I have time to think better of it, I give her a little curtsy. A low chuckle rumbles over my shoulder, and my cheeks flame. *What on earth is wrong with me?*

"Quite the greeting. Do I get one of those too?"

I swing around to face Jace, his handsome face spread in a wide, bemused smile.

"Sorry. Those are only for royalty," I quip, cursing my cheeks for giving away my false show of confidence.

He laughs—a low, rich sound that flows over my body and sends a shiver down my spine. "Understood. In that case, are you ready to get going?" he asks, taking me in slowly with his eyes.

"Oh, she's ready, all right!" Kasey pipes up, scurrying over to me with a pair of strappy black heels in her arms. "Put these on, and you'll be ready to go."

I shoot her an irritated look, knowing she must

have hidden those from me earlier for this very moment. There's no way in hell I'll admit I look like a stumbling baby gazelle in heels in front of him. I'll just have to make the best of it.

I dutifully take the heels from her grasp and begin sliding them on my slender feet, thanking the gods upstairs for giving me the foresight to get a pedicure the other day.

As I rise to my full height, Jace's eyes trail over my bare legs. I gulp, raising my eyes to meet his gaze darkening with barely contained lust.

Damn, I really love this dress. I step closer to him, drunk on confidence as I let my hips sway a little more than I normally would have.

Jace looks at my dress like he would like nothing better than to see it on the floor. Tension swirls as we lock eyes, and my throat bobs at the look in his dark irises.

Kasey clears her throat. "So, uh, yeah. I'm gonna get out of here now. You two lovebirds have fun and don't do anything I wouldn't do!"

I start to say something along the lines of, *that's not a whole lot, you know,* but before I get the chance, she's gone, the slam of the front door confirming her departure.

"I really like this," he mutters, stepping closer to

pinch the hem of my dress between his thumb and forefinger. "It makes you look... bewitching."

I can't help but laugh. "And here I thought you were going to say something normal like *sexy* or *hot.*"

He pauses, his eyes dark and intense on mine. "There's nothing ordinary about you, sunshine. A special woman deserves special adjectives, in my humble opinion."

"Oh, so now it's a *humble* opinion. And here I was under the impression that your ego was the size of Justin Bieber's mansion."

His eyes flash with something like excitement before he lowers his lips to my ear. "Careful, sunshine. Any more of that attitude and I won't be able to stop myself from bending you over my knee."

A small gasp escapes my lips as he chuckles against me before pulling away. "Lucky for you, there's not enough time to make you scream the way I want."

My breath catches in my chest, and whatever I had planned to say melts away on my tongue like shaved ice in summer. I'm not sure whether to be outraged at his confidence or utterly turned on by the prospect of his palm striking my ass.

Faced with that infuriating, cocky smirk of his, I go with the former. "If you want to hear someone scream, I would ask your balls after they meet the toe of my shoe."

"Whatever you say, sunshine." Jace chuckles low in his throat, clearly unfazed by the impending danger to his manhood.

The nerve of this man.

"Yeah, right. If I somehow lose all of my brain cells and give in to every one of your testosterone-fueled impulses, maybe. Until then, not likely," I snap, though I don't quite believe the words as they come out.

Jace seems to want to say more but thinks better of it at the last moment.

"Are you ready to get going? I'm starving."

He says "starving" while raking his eyes over my curves, making me gulp at the thought of him between my legs, getting his fill.

Stop that! I shake my head as a little shiver runs down my spine, my treacherous cheeks warming. Before my sanity dissolves, I step back from him and walk toward the front door, waving for him to follow me.

His footsteps sound close, causing a satisfied smile to form on my face. I'm not sure what the rest of the night has in store, but I'd be lying if I said his promise from earlier doesn't sound appealing.

Damn you, hormones. And damn my last two brain cells that run away whenever he's around.

Chapter Six

I STEAL A GLANCE OUT OF THE CORNER OF MY eye at Jace and shift my weight in the plush leather seats of his Drako GTE. I'm unfamiliar with the make, but Jace spoke the name with pride, so I'm sure it's some expensive, rare model.

It certainly feels that way, at least. With a shiny cherry-red exterior and the comfiest leather seats I've ever had the pleasure to sit my ass on, the whole thing screams "luxurious." Lost in thought, I nearly jump out of my skin when Jace breaks the comfortable silence.

"Penny for your thoughts?" His fingers shift over the gearstick, and I can't help but admire its slim, tapered design. It kind of reminds me of the head of a dildo without all the curves and ridges.

Jesus, is everything in this car an homage to sex?

"My thoughts are *so* not worth a whole penny," I quip. Hell could freeze over, and I still wouldn't tell him what I was just thinking about. Nuh-uh. No way.

"I'd have to disagree," he says, letting go of the shift and snaking it onto my lap.

The feel of his rough palm on my bare thigh warms my core, and I steal another glance at him through lowered lids. I still can't believe this is the same Jace from four years ago. My goofy, platonic best friend Jace. Maybe something in rich people's water makes them more God-like.

A low chuckle rumbles from Jace's throat, and my cheeks warm, realizing I've been hard-core staring at him for the last I-don't-even-know-how-long.

"Okay, now you *have* to tell me what's going on in that pretty mind of yours." He turns from the road to give me a dazzling smile.

Be still, my beating heart.

"Wouldn't you like to know?" I cross my arms across my chest with a grin of my own.

"Yes, that's kind of why I asked."

"Well, it's a secret. And it's definitely nothing about you if that's what you were wondering."

"Mm-hmm, sure." He tightens his grip on my thigh. "That's why you *totally* weren't staring at me with a little puddle of drool coming out of your mouth."

"Ew! I so was *not!*" I cry, consciously wiping my mouth with the back of my hand.

He laughs. It's a full, guttural noise that makes my stupid heart clench.

"Whatever you say, sunshine."

He gives my thigh one last squeeze before putting his hand back on the wheel, and I have to stop myself from letting out a disappointed whine.

We spend the rest of the ride in comfortable silence, letting the soft sounds of the radio roll over us until we pull in front of a large stone building overlooking the ocean. A sleek, freshly waxed porch wrapped around the circumference of the building sported rows of covered tables and outside seating. A large light-blue sign hung over the entrance's French doors, announcing the establishment's name in large, fancy letters.

"La'Oceanic..." I whisper in awe. I never had the slightest idea a place of this caliber existed outside New York or Chicago.

"Have you been here before? I was hoping to take you somewhere new." Though he tries to hide it, I can detect the slightest hint of disappointment in his voice.

I throw back my head in a laugh. The idea of frequenting a place like this is too much for me to bear. When I finally compose myself, Jace stares with a raised brow.

Oh, right. I never answered him.

"Uh... no. I have never ever been to this place or anything like it. The restaurants I go to are strictly in the *single* dollar sign price bracket."

He smiles, his dimples making another grand appearance and causing my knees to go all wobbly.

"Good. I plan to take you to more places like this."

I give him a look out of the corner of my eye. "So... how rich are you, exactly?"

He chuckles, clearly amused by the question as he pulls over to the valet. "Enough to buy you an island. Any other burning questions?"

Before I have time to answer, a gangly boy with acne spots taps on Jace's window.

"Good evening, Mr. Maddox. Want me to take her off your hands?"

My eyebrows shoot to my hairline at the greeting. "Mr. Maddox, huh? You must be a big deal around these parts."

"It is my restaurant, after all. I would be a little put out if no one recognized me," he says with a wink, hopping out of the car and making his way over to my side. He opens the door for me, holding out a large palm for me to balance as I step out.

Snaking his arm around my lower back, he leads me to the double doors, his mouth curved in a tiny smile.

"You know, it is weird." I pause to glance at the handsome man at my side. "I don't remember you being filthy rich when we were friends."

"That's probably because it's a bit of a... new acquisition of mine."

"Are you trying to tell me you won the lottery?"

He chuckles, shaking his head slightly as he pulls the door open for me. "Not the lottery. But a bit of good luck, yes."

I narrow my eyes at him. "Is there a particular reason you're being so cryptic right now?"

He laughs. "No reason. Just thought you'd like to have something to discuss over dinner. We can tell all our secrets now and sit in silence at the table if you'd rather."

I roll my eyes, deciding to let the issue drop for now. He's right. We have all night to learn about each other.

"Mr. Maddox, what a pleasure to see you tonight." A fit, platinum blonde in a sleek black dress gives him a dazzling smile as soon as we step inside. Her eyes flash with irritation when she notices me, and her smile becomes territorial.

"Oh, I didn't realize you brought a guest. So it will be two tonight?" she asks, shooting me a mean little glare as he turns to kiss my temple.

"That's right. Thank you, Annabelle," he says, his voice tight.

She doesn't seem to catch this because her blinding smile returns in full force as soon as he addresses her.

"Right away, sir," she coos, her voice dripping with desire as she gives him a once-over before reaching for two menus behind the podium.

She gestures to us to follow her, and I have to stop myself from rolling my eyes as she glares at me beneath her perfectly cropped bangs. If she wants Jace this badly, there isn't a thing someone like me can do to stop her. She's like Kasey in that way; gorgeous and blond with impossibly long legs and a figure that screams, "I do pilates!" They can have any man they want, while I... apparently have to settle for cheating dickwads like Chaz.

I sneak a glance at Jace out of the corner of my eye —beautiful and masculine and effortlessly blending in with the finery around us—and wonder for the thousandth time what the hell he's doing here with *me*.

"Here you are, sir... ma'am." She turns, showing me her teeth in what she must think is a smile. "Your server will be along shortly. And, *please*..." Her voice lowers to a husk as she turns to address Jace. "Let me know if there is *anything else* I can do for you tonight, *Mr. Maddox*."

My stomach roils as she bats her overly done lashes

at him, but Jace doesn't seem to be paying her any mind. His dark, brooding gaze stays locked on me, slowly trailing over my frame with the same ravenous look.

"Thank you," he clips, never looking away from me. "I don't see what else I would need from you, but I appreciate the offer."

I try—miserably—to hide my satisfied smirk as her face drops. She lets out a huff and stomps off toward the front of the house, showcasing the back of her bright red neck.

Sensing Jace's eyes on me, I snap my head to see him holding out my chair with a bemused little grin.

"Any day, beautiful."

"Oh, right," I mutter, dutifully sliding into my seat. "So... I'm assuming that kind of thing happens often?"

His face tightens as he goes to sit opposite me. "Unfortunately, yes. I've learned that being polite does nothing but spur them on further. So as much as I hate it, I kind of have to be a dick about it sometimes."

"Good God, your shoulders must be *aching* from the weight of that ego you've been carrying around lately."

He grins, his dark eyes lighting with a playful glint. "I don't think you're doing me justice. Also, you're the one who brought it up in the first place, remember?"

My mouth pops open in indignation as a pudgy man in a plain black suit shuffles over to the tableside. He holds a quiet sense of urgency behind his tired eyes, highlighted beneath thinning brown hair that adds at least a decade to his weathered features. This is a man who has dedicated his life to catering to the public. *This* is the head server.

The man eyes my expression suspiciously, probably wondering who let a gaping fish into this fine establishment.

"I... can come back later if you need a few more minutes..."

I snap my mouth shut and give him a tight-lipped smile as my cheeks flame.

"No, that's okay, Paul." Jace smiles easily, his dark eyes shining with amusement as he takes in my expression. "We'll start with a bottle of red. You know the one I like."

"Right away, sir."

The man now known as Paul nods dutifully and shuffles off again, leaving me to face the infuriatingly sexy smirk that Jace gives me across the small oak table.

"Something funny?" I ask, crossing my arms.

His smile grows wider, showing off two perfect dimples. I have to actively pretend they don't make my heart race.

"Not really. I just think you're adorable."

Instead of melting like putty in front of him like my traitorous body wants me to, I straighten my back and roll my eyes.

"I dare you to say I'm adorable when my heel meets your shin under this table."

He holds a broad hand to his chest as his laughter fills the space around us.

"Shit, did I say adorable? I meant unequivocally ruthless." He wipes a fake tear from the corner of his eye.

"Much better," I say, letting out the giggle I'd been holding in.

Just then, Paul returns to us with a bottle and two crystal wine flutes in hand. Placing the glasses in front of us, he pours a small amount of the scarlet liquid into each cup and invites us to taste. Not needing to be told twice, I raise the glass eagerly to my lips and suck the contents down in a single gulp.

Jace's eyes shine with amusement while Paul looks like he physically wants to grab me by the shoulders and shake.

"How did it taste?" Jace asks, his smile widening as Paul actually *flinches.*

"Oh, um... like red wine?" I shrug, holding out my empty glass to Paul with a smile. "I've never met a bottle I didn't like."

Paul gives me a look like he would rather hand over

his firstborn child, and it finally clicks in my mind that it was a *very* expensive cup of grape juice that I just downed.

"I...promise that I will savor this one," I say, giving him as innocent a smile as I could muster.

Paul—or Stingy Wine Man, as I would be calling him from now on—narrows his eyes and grips the bottle tighter to his chest, glaring like I'm some greedy little hobgoblin who's plotting to steal his precious alcohol.

"Go on, Paul. If the lady wants to drink me dry, so be it," he says before downing his own glass.

Paul mutters something under his breath that sounds like *"uncivilized swill"* before giving each of our glasses a hefty pour. He goes to place the bottle on the table and pauses, no doubt wondering whether he could leave such a prized possession in the hands of us miscreants. His job and position clearly winning out over his love of fine wine, he huffs and places it down begrudgingly before trudging away from the table.

As soon as he is out of earshot, I try my luck and take a giant sip of the delicious red wine, wiping the back of my hand across my mouth with a satisfied "Ahhh" as I lower the half-empty glass.

Having taken a mouthful of his own drink, Jace nearly spits it out across the table as I do, his eyes shining with unshed laughter.

"Good lord, woman, are you trying to kill me?" he asks through exaggerated breaths.

"Why would I kill the man supplying me with all this scrumptious wine? That just seems like poor decision-making."

Jace's eyes burn through me as he raises the glass to his lips, pausing before taking a sip to say, "You're right. Much better to kill me in my sleep tonight after I've given you a lifetime of orgasms."

I choke on my wine.

"I'm starting to think we really need to have a talk about the size of that ego," I quip, not even caring that I sound like a broken record as I go to pour myself another full glass.

Whether it was my lame-ass comeback or the fact I seemed determined to down my weight in wine after his comment, Jace—thankfully—drops the subject.

"I know I asked earlier as a joke, but really, how do you like it?" he asks, nodding toward the near empty bottle to my left.

"It's the best glass of wine I've ever had—which isn't saying much, but still. It's really no wonder Mr. Grumpy Wine Man doesn't like me. I guess I haven't been around the *finer* things in life to appreciate them like I should."

He shrugs, making his suit bulge against his biceps and chest in a devastatingly sexy way.

"Paul is a great worker, but his attitude has never been lost on me. He cares *too much* for the finer things. It's good that you don't. I see way too much of that nowadays."

I pause to take in the man across from me—the man who is as good as a stranger to me now, though we had once been the best of friends. So much has happened in such a short amount of time—for us both —and it's really hitting me at this moment.

"I don't mean for this to sound rude or anything, but... what happened to you? I mean, you're like a completely different person. New cars, new clothes, new life. How can so much change in just a few years?"

My eyes shoot to his knuckles wrapped gracefully around the thin stem of his glass, and another thought occurs to me.

"Also, what the heck happened to your hand? You look like you've been beating a wall into submission."

He shakes his head and chuckles darkly into his glass. "Now *that* I thought you'd have the answer to. Don't you remember me pulling that guy off you at the club?"

"Wait, that was *you?*" My mind reels. "Why did you do that?"

He shrugs. "He had his hands on you, and you didn't seem to like it. Drunken assholes respond better to a fist than by asking them to fuck off nicely."

"Is that your 'humble' opinion talking again?"

"No, this is more of an experience thing." He grins before finishing the rest of his glass. "As for your earlier question... I don't really know *what* happened. One day, I was the kid who didn't even have two nickels to rub together. The next..." He swings an arm out, gesturing to all the fineries around us. "It honestly still feels unreal to me."

"So what, you just woke up one day and had millions in your bank account?"

"No, one day, I sold the IP to my invention. *Then* I had millions of dollars in my bank account."

My eyes widen. "What kind of tech sells for that much?"

He grins proudly, showcasing perfectly straight teeth and those damn dimples of his.

"The kind that saves the planet."

Chapter Seven

I BLINK AT HIM SLOWLY, WAITING FOR HIM TO elaborate. After taking a large sip, he does.

"I got the idea from my dad's sanctuary, of all places. Having to go out every day and cut sea animals free from all the trash people dump in the ocean really takes a toll on your view of humanity. Most people don't get to see the damage it does to life, and less than that actually give two shits about it. One day, I got sick of it. I started tinkering in my man's old tool shop, seeing what I could piece together, what worked, and what was shit. Eventually, I came up with something that worked, something that *really* worked. Using a modified buoy device I created, the thing skims over the surface of the water and sucks the floating trash into large, net-like systems that trail the machine for hundreds of feet. When the device is full, it heads back to shore and deposits its collection into designated trash facilities. The thing could run all day, and the amount of garbage I collected in those first few test weeks was... astounding."

His eyes shine with unadulterated pride as he tells me the ins and outs of his multimillion-dollar invention, his face lit with the excitement of a little boy on Christmas morning. It occurs to me that it's probably been some time since he's talked about his most prized achievement.

I want to give him a response that is just as enthusiastic as his description, but all my little pea brain can come up with is, "That's... honestly amazing."

Because it *is*. The man built some multimillion-dollar ocean cleaning machine in his dad's garage over a single summer; he must have been guzzling his Wheaties.

Jace's smile turns bashful at my wondrous expression.

"I appreciate it. It doesn't really feel like it's real yet... like I actually have the power to make a difference in this world now."

Lost somewhere in his own thoughts, I take a moment to gaze around the restaurant again and notice nearly every seat is filled with some well-to-do couple or high-powered business person.

"So why the restaurant? I mean... you started with

tech and wildlife stuff. It's a far cry from the service industry."

Another bashful smile. "I like to tell myself it was because it's a smart business proposition. And it *is*. This place has been profitable for years and gives me the opportunity to expand my portfolio and buy more places for more profit: clubs, bars, motel chains, you name it. But if I'm really honest with myself..."

He stops, looking like he's contemplating whether to say what he's thinking.

"If I'm honest with myself... the first person I thought of when my partner showed me the location was... you."

"Me?" My eyebrows draw together. "What on earth would I have to do with a decision like that?"

His smile falters as he reaches for the bottle of wine. "I don't know if you remember, but there *was* a time when I held your opinion above all else. I guess I still do. And also..." He drags his dark eyes to mine. "The first time I saw this place, I couldn't stop thinking about how much I would like to take you here someday. How your eyes would light up, how regal you would look in the lights and atmosphere of it all. That's how I knew."

The air between us stills, and I swear I can hear my pulse thrumming. What is he saying? That he's waited for me all this time. Pined over me, even?

No, that can't be it, I decide, giving myself an internal shake. *He probably just thought I had good taste and wanted my opinion. We were best friends, after all...*

I'm broken out of my thoughts as Jace chuckles. "I *was* a little presumptuous, that I'll admit. You could have been married with a kid on the way by the time I was buying the thing."

"And you still went ahead with it?"

He gives me a look. "Well... yeah. It was a really good business move."

Okay, now I feel silly.

"Right," I mutter, trying not to think about the way my heart just fell. "Well, you never really had to worry about someone sweeping me off my feet. By the time you were buying this place, I was unhappily in a relationship with some dude who cheated on me relentlessly."

Jace's brows draw together. "He was... cheating... on you..." He says it slowly like he's trying to comprehend some graduate-level physics problem. He throws the rest of his wine back and shakes his head in disgust.

"I don't fucking understand it."

"You and me both," I mutter, following suit with my own glass.

Jace reaches forward and pours the remaining contents of the bottle into our glasses. I can't help but notice mine is a tad bit fuller than his, but I make no comment.

"To reuniting at the right time," he says, holding his glass in the air and tipping it toward me in a toast, "and to that asshole for not realizing what he was fucking up. If it wasn't for his pea brain, I wouldn't have the pleasure of sitting here with the most gorgeous woman in the room."

He rakes his eyes over me hungrily, and I shift in my seat, positive the room has jumped at least thirty degrees.

Nonetheless, I raise my glass to his, praying he doesn't notice the slight shake of my wrist as I tell him, "I'll toast to the first part, but I'll drop dead before I toast to that dunderhead."

His chest shakes with the effort to hold in a chuckle as I tap the rim of my glass to his before draining it in two massive gulps.

"You really haven't changed at all, you know," he says with a hint of adoration in his voice.

"Not all of us have the luxury of becoming billionaires overnight, you know," I quip, trying my best not to notice the warmth emanating from my core. It's really hard not to, considering the starved look darkening the man's eyes.

Luckily, Paul chooses that moment to make his grand, judgmental appearance once again.

"Have you both had time to look over the menu?" he asks, eyeing the *extremely* empty bottle of wine he had left with us mere minutes ago. "Or do you both need more wine—*time?*"

"We would *absolutely* love more wine," I pipe up, enjoying the way Paul's face twists in surprise.

With a wide grin, Jace leans back in his seat and nods in the affirmative to Paul. Without skipping a beat, he snaps his eyes back to me as he asks, "You're not a vegetarian now, are you?"

I don't even think before responding. "No, my love of meat is just as healthy as it's always been."

As soon as the words are out, I know I've messed up. A tiny gasp rattles from Paul's immense chest as Jace coughs and sputters a mistimed sip of wine all over the table.

My entire body warms with the flame of embarrassment as I shift a meek smile from man to man. "Sorry... I didn't mean—"

"Ma'am, it's fine," Paul grunts, looking a little red. "We all know what you meant."

"See, Paul knows what you meant," Jace chimes, grinning a little bit too hard for my taste. "Get this woman the finest and *largest* filet you have back there," he adds with a wink.

I swear to all that is mighty and righteous, if this wasn't such a hoity-toity place, I would reach across the table and smack that maddening smirk right off his face.

Needing no further instruction and obviously desperate to escape, Paul skitters off back to the kitchen without another word. I send a glare Jace's way and cross my arms over my chest.

"Is it your personal mission to make your waitstaff uncomfortable or something?"

"What?" he asks, shrugging innocently. "It was funny! I was just having a bit of fun. No one said he has to be so stuffy all of the time."

I roll my eyes. "Maybe he's that way because he has *you* for a boss. It would drive even the strongest of men mad... literally."

"Impossible," he retorts, scrunching his face as if I suggested the sky is purple. "I'm a wonderful boss, for your information. I'm pretty sure Paul's just made that way."

"A narcissist *would* say that."

His mouth pops open in mock indignation, its effect lessened by the playful sheen swirling in his eyes.

"I prefer self-aggrandizer, thank you very much."

"Of *course* you would prefer some pompous adjective like that. But what you get is narcissistic egomaniac," I retort, though I'm finding it hard to hold back a giggle.

"I feel like that term is a bit excessive... but okay." Jace's dimples pop.

"I'm sorry, did I just imagine the part where I saw you for the first time in years while you were *modeling* for a nude painting class? If anything, I was being merciful."

He shrugs it off, but I swear I see a hint of pink line his cheeks in the dim lighting.

"That was for a good cause. It's not like I do it on a regular basis."

"That doesn't negate the fact that your ego is bigger than this room."

"You're the one on a date with this supposed 'narcissistic egomaniac.' I wonder what that says about you?"

I shrug, trying to remain nonchalant even though I've been asking myself that question damn near the whole night.

"Certainly nothing good... But who knows, maybe I hit my head a little harder than the doctors thought when I got this," I say as I hold my wrist to the light, showcasing the various surgical scars marring the skin there.

In an instant, Jace's face sobers. Reaching forward, he wraps his palm around my wrist and pulls it over the table between us. His eyes darken, and his face twists with what appears to be guilt as he absentmindedly begins rubbing gentle circles around the imperfections with the pad of his thumb.

"Cass, I... I want you to know how sorry I am that I wasn't there." He pauses for a moment before continuing in a soft, tortured voice. "There's really no excuse for it. I should have been by your side when you were going through everything, and I wasn't..." He stops again, looking like he's debating whether he should say whatever's coming next. "I don't want to rehash the past or tell you how much of an idiot I was four years ago because we both know it's true. That night you left, and the fight that we had... it's the biggest regret of my life. The way I spoke to you, I..." He shakes his head. "I'm not even going to try to justify it."

Suddenly, his thumb stops swirling on my palm, and I look up, seeing him caught in some faraway memory.

"When I heard what happened... about you being in the hospital... I wanted to see you more than anything. But I thought—God, it sounds so stupid saying it out loud—I thought that you were better off without me. The way we left things... You deserved a man who was mature and could handle his own emotions. I didn't want to give you any more drama to deal with, so I stayed away. "

He blinks quickly in succession, and if I weren't so

laser-focused, I would have missed the tears welling in the corners of his eyes.

"It's my biggest regret in life," he says, letting out a mournful sigh. "One that I want to spend the rest of my life correcting, if you'll let me."

My chest tightens at the raw emotion spilling out of his words, and I want nothing more than to reach over the table and pull him into me. Right now, he isn't the charming, self-assured, carnal version of Jace I've come to know. He looks *helpless*.

I open my mouth to say something—anything—to let him know he has nothing to worry about. That I'm just as much to blame as he is and that I never want to be apart again.

Of course, before I have time to say *any* of that, Paul makes the most unfortunate of reappearances.

"I have two filets here. Medium rare with a side of seasonal greens and garlic herb potatoes. Plus, more wine," Paul announces as he places the plates in front of us, oblivious to Jace's and my stupefied expressions.

"Thank you... so much," Jace clips, giving Paul a tight-lipped smile.

"Can I get you both anything else?"

Jace raises his brow in a question, but I am simply too stunned to speak, so I just shake my head.

Whether it's my expression or the ridiculous situation, Jace's eyes clear and flash with amusement. His thumb continues its circular motion across the back of my hand, and he looks back over to Paul with shoulders far less tense than they were just moments ago.

"I think we're set. Thanks again, Paul."

"My pleasure."

With that, the man is off again, leaving Jace and me in a staring battle over two heaping plates of meat and potatoes.

"So... what do you say?"

I tilt my head at him, trying my damnedest to resist the urge to dive face-first into the heavenly scented plate of food.

"Uh... to what?" I ask, realizing I still haven't responded.

Jace's chest shakes with a chuckle. "You've already forgotten?"

"It's kinda hard to think over this steak. Have you seen the *size* of this thing?"

Jace's eyes shine with amusement as he asks, "The whole 'giving me another chance' monologue?"

I blink slowly.

"Please tell me it's ringing a bell. I honestly don't know if I have the wind in me to make another heart-felt speech like that."

A slow grin works its way onto my face, and I tell him, as if it's the simplest thing in the world, "After this meal, I'm pretty much prepared to give you anything your little heart desires."

"We'll see about that," he rasps.

Me and my stupid mouth. It might just get me into trouble tonight, after all.

Chapter Eight

"THAT... WAS ABSOLUTELY AMAZING." I SIGH, leaning back into my seat with my hand draped lazily over my stomach.

Three empty bottles of wine and the scraps left from the enormous steak dinner are the only things left littering the tabletop, a feat possible due to my inability to stop stuffing my face with the delicious food.

"I second that." Jace smiles crookedly, his voice slurring slightly as he assumes a similar position to mine. "Dessert?"

"Oh, absolutely *not*," I groan, though I almost take my statement back. I'm sure the dessert here is even better than the food, but I physically cannot fit a single other thing inside my stomach.

Jace tips his empty, crimson-stained glass from side to side, looking deep in thought.

"What's up?" I ask, cringing as my own words slur. *That last bottle probably wasn't the best idea...*

"Well, I was just thinking—"

"Careful, you don't want to hurt yourself."

Jace pauses a beat, narrowing his eyes at me playfully before continuing. "I was just *thinking* that we've both had quite a bit to drink tonight."

"Are you trying to tell me you're an alcoholic, Jace?"

He rolls his eyes. "Are you always this frustrating after a few glasses of wine?"

"A *few?* I think you may need to head back to the first grade, dear, because that count is *way* off." I quip, grinning lazily at him.

He shakes his head in mock frustration. "What I'm trying to say is I don't really feel... comfortable driving home with you while I'm this tipsy."

I gasp. "You're just going to *leave me here?*"

Jace mumbles something incoherent before dragging his eyes back to mine. "No, you silly, silly woman. I'm saying we should just get a room and stay here for the night."

I gasp again, this time leaning forward with my hand clutched over my heart. "Are you trying to strip me of my virtue, Mr. Maddox?"

His eyes darken as he leans into me, a tiny smirk marring his otherwise serious expression.

"Only if you ask me nicely."

My cheeks flame, and I lean back, all too aware I might have just played into a situation I'm not equipped to handle.

"I don't see that happening anytime soon," I mutter, not brave enough to meet his eyes for fear he would see the lie.

Jace chuckles under his breath, clearly not believing my words as he tells me, "You know I wouldn't do anything you wouldn't want, Cassandra. Do you not trust me?"

"Of course I do. It's me I don't trust right now." The words come out before I have time to stop them.

He pauses for a moment, taking in my expression and body language carefully. "Listen, I'm drunk, you're drunk, and there are no Ubers that will get us at this time of night in this area. We can get a room with two beds if that makes you feel more comfortable."

"I think that would, yeah," I say, smiling even though my core screams at me to take back what I just said. The thought of spending the night wrapped in his strong arms is—

No. Stop that right now, traitorous brain. I shake my head. *Just because he's not technically a "stranger" doesn't mean we sleep with him on the first date.*

Although, that plan might just fly out of the window the second he takes his shirt off.

Jace smiles at me easily, clearly unaware of my internal battle. "Perfect. I'll let them know to get a room ready for us."

They only have one bed.

Jace had come back to the table, slightly distraught with the information that they were full for the evening. Except for the honeymoon suite, and that's only available due to a "falling out" of the couple who had booked it.

The bell dings as the elevator doors slide open, and Jace ushers me inside with a hand on my lower back.

"After you, sunshine," he whispers, his dimples making their devilish appearance as his eyes drop to the curve of my ass.

My cheeks flame, but I oblige, trying my best to ignore the violent thrumming in my core as he saunters in next to me.

As soon as the doors slide closed, it's like all the oxygen in the small space is sucked up. Jace angles his body toward me, leaning in close until all my senses are swirling with his scent.

"You can breathe, sunshine. I won't take you in the

elevator." He bares his teeth in a grin, reaching up and sweeping his thumb across my bottom lip. "I promised I would be a gentleman, after all."

My chest shakes with the effort to keep my breathing steady. "I didn't realize you promised anything of the sort." My eyes go wide as his pupils blow. A dark chuckle rumbles in his throat, and he leans in farther until his lips are inches from mine.

"Oh, I didn't? I guess I'm off the hook, then." His warm, minty breath fans my face, and I find my lids drifting as I wait for his lips to touch mine.

The elevator comes to a halt with a *ding,* its doors sliding open to reveal a well-dressed elderly couple. Under the weight of their judgmental stares, I attempt to remove myself from Jace. He chuckles as I squirm aimlessly in his grip, my struggle to distance our bodies only ending with me pressed further into him.

"Jace!" I hiss, planting my hands on his chest.

"Relax," he orders, his voice a low warning in my ear. "Unless you want to give these two a little show, that is."

I still in his arms, not wanting to provoke him with that deadly promise lingering in the air. Jace lets out a low, satisfied hum and rests his chin on the top of my head, wrapping his massive arms around me, effectively cutting me off from the wary eyes of the couple.

At the next stop, they practically sprint to get off

the elevator, looking back at our public display with matching scowls fixed on their mouths.

"A picture lasts longer, you know!" Jace calls, drawing a flustered gasp from the woman.

I push my face into Jace's chest, hoping they can't hear the fits of giggles flowing from my mouth as the doors close.

"You liked that?" Jace grins, his eyes alight with a mischievous twinkle.

"I did." I laugh, wiping a tear from my eye. "You almost gave that poor woman a heart attack."

He shrugs, crushing me to his chest as he nuzzles his face into the side of my neck. "Serves them right. It's not my fault they haven't felt anything in their nethers since the First World War."

I laugh, smacking his chest lightly with my palm. "That's horrible."

He shrugs again, loosening his grip so he can look down at me, his eyes burning with a tenderness I've never seen before.

I'm not sure if it's bravery from the wine or the invigorating feeling of being sucked into this man's orbit, but I'm suddenly overcome with emotion. I stare at him, my eyes wide and mouth slightly parted.

It doesn't matter that this is Jace, my best friend since childhood. It doesn't matter how nervous he makes me or how much I want to run from this feeling. I need him to kiss me, to make me his. I was stupid to think I haven't felt this way all along.

Like a giant *fuck you* from the big guy in the sky, the elevator *dings* again. I want to scream in frustration as Jace lets his arms fall from my waist, pausing for a moment to take in my furious features before he walks out onto the carpeted hallway.

"You coming?" he calls over his shoulder, eyes alight with amusement when he notices me frozen in place.

"Yeah, yeah," I mumble, shaking my head as I stomp after him down the hall to our room.

Stopping in front of the dark oak door, he grabs the plastic key card out of his pocket and slides it into the slot, throwing it open for me as soon as the lock clicks open.

I gasp as I step into what is, without a doubt, the nicest hotel room I have ever laid eyes on. A huge king-sized bed takes up the middle of the room, covered with a plush white duvet that contrasts perfectly with the red rose petals strewn across the covers and floor.

Across from the bed are floor-to-ceiling windows that look out over the ocean, complete with a sliding glass door and a ginormous balcony that looks like it wraps around the entirety of the suite.

Taking advantage of my distracted awe, Jace stops

by the edge of the bed, his back to me as he begins stripping off his tie and shirt.

"Whoa! Whatcha doing there, mister?" I ask, unable to help my eyes from roaming over the muscles straining through the thin white shirt covering his back.

"What does it look like?" he responds, swiveling to face me as he pops the last button of his shirt open. My brain is already fuzzy from the wine, but the sight of Jace's bare abs make the room start to spin.

"Uh, trying to seduce me?" *God, I hope there isn't drool on my chin right now.*

He laughs one of his signature, throaty chuckles as he drags his eyes over my frame. The way he roves over every curve agonizingly slowly makes me gulp, prompting another chuckle to fall from his lips.

"Trust me, sunshine. You would know if I was trying to seduce you."

I try to ignore the way my stomach flips as he runs his tongue over his bottom lip, still staring at me with that impossibly hungry look.

I pop my hip, placing my hand on it as I raise a defiant brow. "Is that so?"

He nods, stalking toward me with an expression I can't place. I take a step backward, my eyes going wide as my stiletto rolls sideways into the carpet, threatening to send me crashing to the ground.

Jace is quicker, though. Faster than I can blink, he lunges toward me, gripping my shoulders in his strong, calloused palms before pulling me into his chest.

His hand moves slowly to the back of my head, where he stops, caressing my long black tresses and holding me against him like something he wants to cherish. I allow my eyes to drift close and breathe him in, the familiar scent of cedar and spiced cologne making me feel at home.

Jace's hold loosens enough for me to pull back and look up at him. He brings a hand to my face, lightly running his thumb over my cheekbone. There's some deep, indiscernible look in his dark eyes that I'm not even going to try to unpack right now.

"God, you're so beautiful, Cassandra," he mumbles. My heart rate spikes as I stare at him dumbly. *Oh, that's what he was thinking.*

Before I have time to come up with a response, Jace leans down, crashing his lips onto mine like a man starved. My heart threatens to beat its way out of my mouth as I kiss him back, letting out a tiny moan as his tongue sweeps across my bottom lip. I open, and his tongue dances with mine, drawing some more unlady-like sounds from my parted lips.

When he finally releases me, we're both panting and disheveled, and my core burns frantically for more of him.

With a dark gleam in his eye, Jace smirks. "Like I said—you'd know if I was trying to seduce you."

My mouth pops with indignation. "What the fuck, Jace? You did all this so you could prove a point?"

He frowns, pulling me flush against him while I struggle to free myself from his impossible grip. He leans next to my ear, shielding his face from my view as he whispers, "You have no *idea* how long I've waited to have you. So yes, I'm going to prove a point. You've never been fucked the way you should, sunshine, and that's a damn shame. One I'm going to be correcting tonight."

He pulls back to look at me, and the look in his eyes has all the oxygen leaving my lungs. It's dark and... possessed.

Before my brain can form a response, Jace's mouth crashes down on mine again, forcing any kind of coherent thought from my mind. Sliding his hand up my arm, he fingers the thin strap holding my dress in place before deftly sliding it from my shoulder. Cupping my breast in his palm, he begins teasing my nipple between his thumb and forefinger, rolling and playing with me until I'm about to scream.

"Jace, please," I moan, pressing further into his palm. "I need more."

"And you'll get it," he murmurs against my mouth. "Just be patient."

I start to make a little cry of disappointment that gets cut off as soon as Jace brings his mouth over my breast. I arch my head back in a moan as he takes my nipple between his teeth, nibbling gently and flicking the tip of his tongue across the tight peak. With his free hand, he slips the strap from my other shoulder and rips the hem below my ass in one swift movement before moving on to my other breast.

Slipping my fingers into his dark locks, I ball my hands into fists and grin at the hiss of pleasure that rumbles from Jace's throat. In return, he gives a hard nip to the top of my mound, drawing a gasp of pain mixed with pleasure from my mouth.

"I can play rough, too." Jace smirks at me through impossibly long lashes. "I just hope you're ready for it."

Without waiting for a response, Jace sweeps a hand behind my kneecaps and hoists me into his arms as if I weighed less than a paperweight. He takes two strides toward the bed, looks at me with that evil, dimpled grin of his, then tosses me onto the mattress as easily as he scooped me up.

"Jace!" I squeal. "What on earth was that fo—"

The last word of my sentence gets cut off as Jace lunges toward me, encasing my body under his as he crushes his mouth onto mine. Words, sense, dignity; all of it gets wiped from my mind as soon as Jace touches me, and tonight I want to see just how much he can make me forget.

Bracing with one arm, he slides his hand slowly down my stomach and toward my core while his tongue works its magic in my mouth. His fingers dance lightly along the skin of my inner thigh, swirling and teasing closer to my center but never fully touching me where every nerve in my body begs him to. After too many minutes of his relentless torture, I buck my hips into his palm, hoping that would be enough for him to give me more.

Sensing my desperation, Jace chuckles deep in his chest and moves his fingers farther from my core.

"No!" I whine, bucking my hips against him again, no matter how ridiculous I knew I looked. *I need more, dammit. Why won't you give me more?*

As if in answer to my unspoken question, Jace leans his mouth over to my ear, his voice hauntingly seductive as he whispers to me, "Now, what do you say if you want something?"

My brows tug together, my mind and senses far too muddled to come up with an answer to his question. "What? Jace, just touch—"

"You say please," he growls, a hint of malice entering his tone. "Preferably with a sir at the end since you seem to have forgotten your manners."

I let out a giggle. "Jace, I'm not calling you s—ow!"

Before I can even get the rest of my sentence out, Jace flips me onto my side and delivers a harsh blow to my ass.

"What was that you were saying?" Jace coos, massaging the area he smacked. "You're not going to... what was that again?"

"Nothing," I grumble as he continues rubbing away the sharp stinging sensation.

"Nothing what?"

"Nothing, *sir.*"

"Good girl." I can hear the grin in his voice as he snakes his hand back to my center. "Now... is there something else you were going to ask for?"

His fingers tease the edge of my panties, and I can't think.

"Please," I whisper, bucking my hips as he rubs my clit over the silk. "Please, sir. Please touch me."

Jace chuckles, slipping a single finger past the edge of my panties. "That wasn't so hard, was it?"

He dips his finger into me, swirling it gently along my walls before pulling out to circle the tip around my clit. He repeats this process for an achingly long time, circling my clit gently to bring me to the peak of my release before ripping it away to dive back inside me. I do everything my fuzzy mind can think—I buck my hips, I whine, I plead with him, I barter—but he just smirks at me, refusing to give in.

He brushes me one more time, and I can't take it anymore. One last, violent cry of frustration pours from my mouth as Jace pulls his hand away, only for it to be replaced with a moan of pleasure as he lowers his mouth onto my pussy. His tongue dives into my core, flicking against my walls achingly slowly before releasing me with a moan of his own.

"Jesus... you taste fucking amazing," he growls, staring at me with pupils the size of saucers.

Without giving me a moment to breathe, he lowers his mouth onto me again, feverishly sucking and flicking his tongue against my clit. Jace grips the sides of my hips, holding me to him and refusing to budge as my body shudders with each lash of his tongue.

With one last, gentle pulse against my clit, I explode. Stars spring behind my eyes as I cum, riding wave after wave of pleasure while Jace continues to pulse his tongue against me, coaxing me to the very end.

"Holy shit," I curse, eyes closed and spread limply across the bed. "I think you just made me see God."

Jace's laugh rumbles darkly in his chest. "There's no God in this bed tonight, sweetheart. Only me."

In one swift movement, Jace rips his belt from his waist before reaching down to free his cock from his black dress pants. With wide eyes, I switch my glance from his cock to his face, wondering just how in the hell he'll fit inside me.

Jace grins at me while stroking his length, seeming to know *exactly* what I was thinking. "Don't worry sunshine." He chuckles darkly. "It'll only hurt for a second."

"That's not... I'm still a..." My words get caught in my throat. If I tell him I'm still a virgin, will he back out of this? I know a lot of guys don't want to deal with the kind of responsibility that comes with being someone's first.

"You're still what?"

"I... I haven't really done this before." My neck heats with mortification. *Shit, he's definitely not going to go forward with this, now. I can't even say the word out loud.*

"Are you trying to tell me you're a virgin?"

Instead of the dismissiveness I expect, Jace's voice is filled with wonder. I gaze at him through my lashes, nearly choking at the raw desire swirling in his irises.

"It's okay, sunshine. We don't have to do anything tonight." He leans down, brushing his lips against mine.

"No! That's not what I mean... I want you. I've... *always* wanted you." The last past is barely a whisper, but Jace's eyes fly open as loud as if I'd screamed it.

And it's true. I don't know what took me so long

to realize it, but the reason I've never been interested in having sex with another man, is because the man I've wanted has been here all along. Until he touched me tonight, I was too scared to admit it. But now... now I want to scream it from the top of a damn skyscraper. *I want Jace Maddox.*

Jace's muscles tense as he presses his lips to mine. "Are you sure?"

Breathless from the kiss, I nod, and Jace pulls away. My anxiety flares as the sound of a condom ripping fills the room, but I don't have time to think about it as Jace positions himself between my thighs. Fear blazes into a burning need as Jace the tip of his cock against my slit, coating the head in my arousal.

He cups my cheek in a calloused palm, his dark gaze taking hold of me as he presses his length slowly inside.

"Fuck!" I hiss, digging my nails into his shoulder as the fullness takes me over. My eyes water as he pushes deeper and deeper into me, but it feels too good to stop.

"That's a good girl," he coos, moving slowly in me. "Take all of this cock."

Can't you see I'm fucking trying? I squeeze my eyes shut tight, digging my fingernails so hard into his skin I'm sure to draw blood. Jace either doesn't notice or doesn't care, continuing to slide in and out of me slowly and making sure I feel every single inch of his massive cock.

"Fuck," he moans, the vein in the side of his neck throbbing as he tilts his head back. "I don't know how much longer I can hold back."

Without any other warning, Jace slams into me, knocking the breath from my lungs as I'm filled past anything I've ever felt before.

He fucks me hard, slamming into my walls and rocking his hips with mine until I can barely remember my own name. Just when I think I'm about to explode, he rips his cock out of me, drawing a desperate cry from my mouth.

Jace strokes his length, his bare chest and abs glistening as he hovers above me. In one swift movement, he flips me over onto my stomach before repositioning his cock at my entrance. Desperate to be full of him again, I wiggle my ass into him, pushing back against his hips in an attempt to put him back inside.

Jace leans his mouth close to my ear, pressing the full weight of his chest onto my back as he whispers, "I'm going to fuck you again, harder. You're going to come for me like the good girl you are, and then I'm going to finish. Understand?'

I nod wordlessly, which earns me a sharp slap on my ass.

I whimper while Jace massages the sore area, his

voice deadly when he finally speaks again, "What do you say?"

"Yes!" I cry, desperately trying to wriggle out from under him.

Smack!

"What do you fucking say?"

"Yes, sir," I mumble into the bed, my eyes watering from the sting.

Smack!

"Ow! I said sir that time!" I cry, trying to angle my head back to glare at him.

Two more stinging hits land, followed by a dark chuckle as I cry out.

"Please, sir," I grit through my teeth, not sure if my tears are from pain or humiliation. "Please fuck me."

"Much better," Jace coos, dragging his tongue lightly down my spine. "Much, *much* better."

I cry out as he shoves his full length into me. He fucks me harder and harder, angling his cock so it rubs against my walls in just the right way, and stars spark behind my eyes. When I don't think I can get any higher, he reaches his hand under me and toys with my clit, rubbing and swirling the sensitive nub while he sinks his teeth into my shoulder. His hands, his cock, his mouth—all of it is too much to bear, and I can't hold on any longer.

A cry tears from my mouth as my orgasm rips

through me, causing every muscle in my body to tremble as I ride wave after wave of pleasure. Jace coaxes it out of me, starting to move more slowly and easing up on the intensity of his fingers. Then with one last powerful thrust, his cock throbs inside me with his own release.

Jace rolls off me, taking my body with him as he rolls onto his back, his chest heaving with effort as he catches his breath. I snuggle my head into the crook of his neck, breathing in the smell of sandalwood and musk as I let my eyes flutter closed. The last thing I remember is Jace holding me to his chest, placing delicate kisses across my forehead as sleep finally takes hold of me.

Chapter Nine

THE MORNING LIGHT STREAMS IN THROUGH slits in the dark velvet curtains, waking me from one of the most pleasant dreams I've had in a while. I let out a bear-like groan and throw one of the dense hotel pillows over my face, hoping that would stop some of the assault on my senses. My head is pounding, my mouth feels like I've eaten sand for breakfast, and I reek of sex.

It's the last thought that sends me shooting straight up in bed. I let out a little shriek as the sheet falls from my torso, causing my nipples to pebble when exposed to the chilly air. Pulling the sheet over my chest, I look around the room in confusion.

Jace is nowhere to be found.

Like the poster child I am for overthinking things, I immediately start running through all the worst-case scenarios in my little pea brain. *Maybe he didn't enjoy last night as much as I did? Maybe he thought it was a mistake? Oh God, what if he hates me now?*

My mini freak-out only lasts for a few more moments before the door swings open to reveal the missing man in question. My eyes light when I see what he's holding in his hands.

"Oh, you beautiful, beautiful man," I praise, my mouth watering at the scent of freshly brewed coffee. I pause, my gaze shooting to the side. "I got a little worried when you weren't in bed this morning. I thought—"

"That I left?" His eyes twinkle with amusement. "How could I, when I have a goddess in my bed? A goddess who let me fuck her last night." My cheeks flame, and he shakes with a chuckle as he makes his way over to the bed, sitting at the foot before offering me my morning crack.

"I wasn't sure if you still get the same order, but... that's what I got you." He smiles sheepishly before taking a sip of his own.

"Honestly, you could have handed me a cup of black sludge, and I would drink it with a smile."

"I love it when the bar is set low for me." He takes a sip and winces. "Ugh. Foul."

"I love it." I grin, taking a large sip of my own. "I guess everything's just better when you're around."

"Cassandra Stone." His eyes twinkle. "Is that a compliment I hear?"

I let out a squeal as he lunges for me, piping coffee sloshing over the sheets with the movement. His mouth descends on my neck, nipping and sucking the delicate skin as his hand paws my breast.

"Jace," I moan, my head falling back as a wave of heat shoots to my core. "Jace, I have work today."

If he hears me, he makes no inclination. A trail of fire follows his lips across my collarbone and down my abdomen, adding kindling to the raging fire in my veins.

"Fuck me," I hiss, my knees spreading subconsciously to allow him further access.

"That's exactly what I'm trying to do." A chuckle rumbles in his chest as he places a kiss just above my clit. "You're the one who's trying to stop me from having breakfast."

My throat bobs as his eyes meet mine, the hunger displayed clearly in his dark irises.

"You're going to make me late," I whisper, bucking my hips to meet his mouth.

"I know."

His mouth covers my clit, and Jace works his magic between my legs.

So what if I get fired? Right?

Leaning both elbows on the bartop counter, I let out a yawn so big I contemplate calling the folks from Ripley's Believe It or Not to report it.

I let out a little chuckle at the stupid joke before my manager's scowl comes around the corner, effectively quashing any joy in the small space.

"It's really quite rude not to cover your mouth when you yawn, Cassandra." She sniffs down her witchy nose before reaching to wipe a finger across the counter in front of the espresso machine.

A deep eleven appears between her unkempt brows as she pulls the pad closer to inspect the specks of coffee grounds that dot her fingertip. My eye twitches with the effort to remain silent as she shakes her head with the same disgust as if she's just dragged her hand through a rotting pile of fish guts.

A long silence ensues, and one look at her stubborn expression tells me I'm going to have to be the one to break it.

Taking a deep breath to curb my irritation, I tell myself for the thousandth time to approach her as I would some heated man-eating fish.

"Miranda?" I question gently, making sure to keep sufficient space between the two of us in case she decided to lash out. "Is everything okay?"

The Barracuda whirls her body to face me, her eyes red with the effort of holding in her fury.

"'*Is everything okay?*'" she parrots back, mocking me in a high-pitched valley girl voice that I immediately take offense to.

My fists curl at my side, but I refuse to take her bait. She's been increasingly overbearing these last few months, and I've been growing more and more sure that she's looking for a reason to let me go. It doesn't make a whole lot of sense, considering my work ethic. But I've also heard rumblings of the corporation closing chains left and right, so maybe that has something to do with it.

If she does end up firing me, I can't say I'd be terribly upset. I just wish she wouldn't be such an asshole leading up to it.

When I remain silent, she only seems to grow more enraged, "How can you even ask me that question? Do you *really* not see the state of these counters?"

As if to prove her point, she thrusts her pointer finger in front of my face with a look of sick satisfaction in her eyes, displaying exactly three tiny black specks of espresso.

I don't know if it's the lack of sleep or the lack of fucks I have left to give, but at that moment, I snap.

"It's coffee," I say, my tone audibly hostile. "This is a coffee *shop*. There's going to be coffee *grounds* on the counters sometimes. You know damn well I keep this place spotless, yet you constantly find reasons to be a bitch to me."

Miranda's mouth falls open at my use of the word bitch, but I carry on unfazed.

"I don't get paid *nearly* enough to stand here and take this for one second longer. So you know what? I won't. I quit." I bare my teeth at her in a nasty little sneer as I rip my apron over my head.

From behind my shoulder, the sounds of slow clapping fill the room. Miranda and I whip our heads toward the noise, having been so caught up in our altercation that neither noticed a customer walking in.

"Good for you, sweetie." Though slightly shaky with age, the voice of the woman behind the counter rings out crystal clear in the silence. "I wish I had the balls to stand up to my boss like that when I was your age. Guy was a real wanker."

My mouth pops in surprise, and I notice Miranda's face purpling with rage out of the corner of my eye, but neither of us utters a sound.

"And you..." The woman turns her misty eyes toward my manager, and I have to stifle a chuckle at the raw indignation swimming in them. "How *dare* you speak to this young lady like that. Every time my husband and I have come here, she has been *nothing* but polite and gracious. Even going so far as to remember our orders and the fact that he's allergic to dairy! *You,* on the other hand," she sneers, "well, let's just say I can't say the same kind things about you."

Miranda opens her mouth to speak, but the woman holds a bony finger up to her with an expression so fierce it causes the Barracuda's words to die in her throat.

Satisfied with her silence, the woman turns back to me with a kind smile, "You go on, dear. You have so much life left to live. Best not to waste it in the presence of snakes like her."

The comparison to an equally deadly animal makes me laugh, and I give the woman a smile of thanks as I start to collect my things. The Barracuda watches my every move silently, but thankfully makes no move to stop me or convince me otherwise.

As the door closes behind me, I take a moment to breathe in the salty ocean air, grateful for the random stranger's kindness and reveling in my newfound freedom.

Pulling out my phone as I make my way across the boardwalk, my thumb hovers over Jace's name as I contemplate whether to call him. He reminded me this morning that he would be away from his phone in meetings all day, and the last thing I want to do is get him in trouble with some big executive or something.

With my mind made up, I scroll to Ethan's number and call him.

"What up, twerp?" answers the gruff voice. "You need bail money or something?"

I roll my eyes, but can't help the smile from creeping onto my face at the sound of his voice. If no one else could, my idiot brother always managed to make me feel better. Or, less like the world is caving in, that is.

"I'm just going to ignore that last part," I grumble. "Can't I ever just call you to say hi?"

"Well, yeah... but it's never *just* for that." Ethan chuckles.

"You're a jerk, you know that?"

"Most people would call that observant, but go off," he replies, amusement dripping from his voice. "So what's the problem? Whose ass do I need to obliterate?"

"That literally sounds so wrong, Ethan," I groan, slapping my palm roughly against my forehead as he cackles on the other end of the line.

"You need to get your mind out of the gutter, Cass. And stop stalling."

"Ugh, fine," I mutter, lowering my voice to a near whisper as I tell him, "I kind of...quit my job."

An uncharacteristic amount of silence falls between us.

"Ethan?" I ask, wondering if the call dropped or something. "You still there?"

"Yeah, I'm here." Ethan sighs. "I honestly... I don't know what to say. I'm just... really proud. "

At this, I balk, blinking several times in succession as my brain tries to form words to reply. "You... you're *proud?*"

His laughter rings out through the speaker. "Yeah, I am. Is that so hard for you to believe?"

"Well, no... It's just not the reaction I was expecting, is all."

"Cass, listen." Ethan sighs, his voice taking on that deadly serious, concerned older brother tone he loved to use so much. "Ever since the accident, you've been moping around this town. It's like someone just told you pumpkin spice was outlawed. And before you say anything, let me clarify. It's understandable for you to mourn and take time to figure your shit out. But going back to work at that place has been crushing you, making you into some dejected, cynical, weary shell of a person. One I haven't been able to recognize since your injury. I'm proud of you, Cass, because today you decided to live for you again. Not everyone can do that."

My eyes mist with unshed tears as I think of how to respond to such a heartfelt sentiment from a man usually so reserved.

"That... was literally so fucking cheesy." I can't help but laugh as the first of many tears spills down my cheek.

"Oh, shut up," he grumbles, unable to help the amusement from slipping into his tone. "You're just jealous because I'm more in touch with my emotions than you."

"And I suppose I have a certain redhead to thank for that?" I giggle, thinking of the countless nights Amelia must have spent trying to get him to open up.

"That woman could get a rock to talk about their emotions, I swear." He huffs. "I guess that's one of the reasons I love her so much."

"Oh my God, then hurry up and marry her already, you big baby," I tease, glad we're moving on from the previous subject. I love my brother dearly, but talking to him about my failed dreams and aspirations is not on the list of things I want to do right now.

"Already bought the ring. Shit cost me an arm and a leg to get the one she was eyeing." He sighs at the reminder of his damaged wallet. "Don't you dare go and spoil it for her now that you know." His voice grows stern. "You have no idea the hoops I've had to jump through to keep this thing a secret from her. That woman's ability to figure shit out would make the CIA jealous."

I can't help but laugh. Ethan never learned the art

of being discreet, and I know there's no way in hell he's managed to keep this a secret from her. If I had to guess, she's scouring their apartment right now to find his hiding place.

"I can't believe you're getting married!" I squeal. "Wait, I *am* going to be your best man, right?"

"You'll have to take that up with Amelia. I'm pretty sure I get zero say in the matter."

"Smart woman," I chirp giddily. "I'm so happy for you, E."

"You know what? Me too." He sighs, and I can hear his smile through the phone. "Now we just have to work on you."

"About that..."

"Oh my God, Cass. Please tell me you did not give that hedgehog-looking motherfucker a second chance."

"Of course I didn't!" I snap, an image of Chaz's gelled hair flitting into my mind and making me giggle. "It's someone else... someone you like."

"No... Not Mrs. Butterwraith?"

"My third grade teacher? Really, Ethan?"

A booming laugh sounds from his end of the line. "I'm still holding out for the day you tell me you're a lesbian."

"You're impossible." I palm my forehead. "No, you idiot, it's Jace. Jace Maddox."

Silence.

"Helloo? Did I lose you?"

"Did you sleep with him?" he asks, his voice soft.

I don't answer.

"I'm going to fucking kill him!" Ethan bellows.

"What? No! What the hell, Ethan!"

"He was supposed to be my eyes and ears when I'm not around. He wasn't supposed to stick his gear shift inside you."

"His *gear shift?* Are you twelve?"

"That is so not the point, Cassandra!" he bellows. "I'm going to fucking kill him. You were supposed to wait until you were married, dammit!"

I roll my eyes, hard. Ethan has always been so damn overprotective. He and Jace were the main reasons growing up that I never got close enough to a guy to sleep with him. It was silly of me to think he'd respond differently, even for Jace.

In any case, It's amazing to see how quickly he can go from carefree to downright murderous. "Jace is treating me *very* well, so there will be no more talk of unaliving," I tell him sternly.

"Fine. But the minute he fucks up, I'm teaching him a lesson," he grumbles. His words are followed immediately by a loud crashing in the background, and I pull the phone away with wide eyes.

"Ethan? You okay?" I call, my heart hammering against my chest wall.

"Sorry, Cass, gotta go." I'm barely able to make out his voice from all the commotion in the background. "Some guy just dropped an entire load of pallets off the side of the truck. Fucking idiots, I swear."

Without another word, he ends the call. I roll my eyes. *Men.*

I look at my blank screen for a moment before opening it to type a message to Kasey.

ME

> Guess who just quit their job and needs to get drunk to forget about it?

KASE

> You're JOKING. Helllsss yes, I'm so down.

ME

> You always are ;p Meet me at my place in a few hours?

KASE

> It's a date <3

I look at the message from Kasey ordering me to "get my sexy ass outside," and suck in a deep breath before giving myself a final once-over in the mirror. Smoothing my hands across the sleek satin material of my new black cowl-neck minidress, I can help but feel a little spark of pride. *I do look damn good...if only Jace was around to see it.*

My face crumples with an intense spark of longing that follows the thought of him, and I turn from the mirror. Forcing the feelings down, I slip on a pair of chunky black heels and make my way out the door to Kasey's Mustang.

"Goddamn, way to show a girl up, Ms. Sexy thang." Kasey whistles from the driver's seat as I slide into the car.

I let out a dry laugh before rolling my eyes at her. "That would literally be impossible. But thank you."

Kasey scoffs before yanking the shift into drive and turning onto the main road.

"You know, I thought having a literal billionaire Greek god fawn over you would give you some more confidence, but you're still just as delusional as ever."

At the mention of Jace, the same pang from earlier rips through my chest. I look at my phone, hoping for a word from him, but am greeted by nothing but a blank screen. Not wanting to ruin the mood with my clear codependency issues, I quickly change the subject to get my mind off the man in question.

"So...where is it we're going exactly?" I ask, angling my body in the seat to face her.

Kasey keeps her eyes on the road, but I see a small smirk begin to creep along the side of her mouth.

"Oh, just a fabulous new bar that may or may not be invite-only," she announces coyly, "And—drum roll, please—your best friend knows a way to get us in!"

She sounds so excited to tell me that I plaster a big fake smile on my face to try to match her energy. Just because I don't care about exclusive clubs and experiences doesn't mean I can't pretend for her sake.

"That's so rad!" I tell her, my cheeks beginning to fatigue from the effort of holding the grin.

Kasey rolls her eyes. "You know, that'd be a little more believable if you weren't using words that were last heard in the sixties. But it doesn't really matter, because we're already here."

As Kasey pulls her car into one of the last parking spots lining the street, I peer out the window and immediately spot a huge line of people flooding the sidewalk in front of what I can only assume is the bar in question. The Red Letter is displayed above the door in neon red letters, casting an ominous glow onto the scowling features of the ex-linebacker-looking bouncer.

I turn to Kasey to ask if she's sure we're going to be let in, but my eyes are met with an empty seat and the slam of the driver's side door.

Letting out a small huff, I turn and hop out,

watching her slender frame sashay straight over to the gruff-looking man guarding the entrance. I watch in amusement as his stony expression falters as soon as she presents him with her dazzling smile and a flutter of her long, dark lashes.

She straightens to whisper something next to his ear, and his eyes jerk to me as I amble toward them. His eyes run over my curves slowly before he turns his attention back to Kasey, giving her a gruff nod and a wave with his fingers.

With a chirp of excitement that cuts through the busy night air, Kasey swings an arm over my shoulder and practically shoves me through the door and into a dimly lit foyer. Out of the corner of my eye, I notice the bouncer shaking his head, his chin tucked to his massive chest that's shaking with a chuckle.

Once I'm positive we're far enough out of earshot, I ask her, "Should I even ask what it was you said to make the scary man's eyes go all googly?"

"Hmm? What do you mean?" She bats her lashes at me innocently, which only serves to make her look anything but. "I just asked him nicely if he would let us skip the line. What's the big deal?"

"Mmm, sure." I narrow my eyes at her dubiously but decide it's probably better for my sanity if I let the issue drop. "Let's just get a drink before I regret this decision."

"Don't be such a party pooper." Kasey rolls her eyes but still takes my hand and leads me toward the bar, which, to my surprise, is behind a secret door hidden within the bookcase lining the entire back wall.

"After you." She grins, ushering me in with an unmistakable air of giddiness in her voice.

I step inside, blinking in quick succession as my eyes adjust to the darkened loft-style space. A massive oak bar lines the right-hand side of the room, positioned expertly in front of a wall of liquor that goes so high up that it has a twentysomething-foot ladder installed so employees can reach the upper shelves. Toward the back, an industrial stairwell leads to an open second story, which houses the band, who are playing some sensual alternative rhythm I've never heard before.

"Holy shit," I whisper in amazement, gazing around dumbly at the sheer amount of people who fill the dance floor and surrounding space.

"Pretty awesome, right?" Kasey tugs on my wrist. "Come on, you said you wanted a drink, right?"

"Oh, there's nothing I would like more." I sigh with relief as I follow her lead toward the monumental wall of alcohol, which is surrounded by more people than the walls can hold bottles for.

Undeterred, Kasey saunters past a tightly packed

group of college-aged boys straight to the counter. After a few moments of conversation and lash fluttering, the bartender drops what he's doing before and turns from the rest of the crowd. He returns seconds later with a dopey grin on his face and proudly hands her two hefty cups of amber liquid while the rest of the waiting patrons look on with both shocked and slightly enraged expressions.

I roll my eyes but am unable to stop the smile that toys at my lips.

Ladies and gentlemen, my absolute siren of a best friend. I giggle as she sashays back over to me, a haughty smile of her own splayed across her face.

"For you, my dear. Here's to an amazing night out!" She cries, holding her plastic cup out to cheers before tilting her head back and downing the entire thing.

With wide eyes I follow suit, spluttering and coughing once the last drop of liquid passes my tongue.

"For fuck's sake," I choke, cupping my throat that feels like it's in the seventh circle of hell. "You could have warned me that we were about to chug an entire cup of straight up *bourbon,* you know."

She shrugs. "Yeah, but then you wouldn't have done it with me. So..." Giggling, she reaches for my hand and leads me toward the throng of sweaty strangers crammed together on the dance floor.

Though I don't know the lyrics to the songs the band is playing, each one has a good beat, and we have no problem dancing around like idiots for a few songs before Kasey decides we need another round of "dancing juice."

I step off to the side to catch my breath as her blond updo disappears within the huddled masses, then reach into my pocket to check my phone.

My heart thunders against my rib cage as my eyes take in a new message from Jace, and I quickly reprimand myself for acting like such a lovestruck teenager.

JACE

> Thinking of you <3 Can't wait to be back in bed together

Dragons roar to life in my belly at the little words displayed on my screen, and I don't even realize the shit-eating grin that's made its way onto my face before Kasey stumbles to me.

"Damn, that must be some dick pick for you to be smiling at your phone like that."

Immediately, the grin drops from my face, and I wrinkle my nose at her. "That's literally so gross, Kase."

"What?" She shrugs innocently before thrusting another overflowing cup into my hand. "Respect the penis, babes."

Thanks to an ill-timed sip, I choke on my drink.

"You should have seen your face." Kasey cackles, doubled over while I fight for my life.

"I..." *Cough.* "Can't..." *Cough.* "Stand you." I gasp, my eyes watering from the liquor that made its way up my nose.

Still giggling, Kasey shimmies toward the center of the dance floor, waggling her fingers at me in a come-hither motion and grinning like a maniac. I take a hefty sip from my cup to soothe my throat, then stumble after her to continue dancing the night away.

Several drinks later, Kasey and I are slick with sweat and just about ready to throw the towel in when I see her eyes lock on something over my shoulder.

"Don't look now, but I think I see your man candy back there," she says, her words slurring slightly with every syllable.

"Who? Jace?" I ask, whipping my head in the direction she's looking.

"Oh my God, I told you not to look," Kasey groans, slapping her palm to her forehead with a little too much force and wincing.

"We're *so* taking an Uber home tonight." I shake my head at her as I see her mouth pop open to protest.

"There's no way either of us are getting behind that wheel tonight, Ms. Drunky."

"Fine." She pouts. "Can't Jace drive us home, though? I really think they'll kick me off the app if I throw up in one more person's car."

"God, you're a mess," I groan. "And I guess I can ask, but... he said he was working this weekend. I don't want to bother him if he's busy."

"Uh, he doesn't look all that busy," Kasey mutters, her eyes focused somewhere over my shoulder.

"What do you mea—" My words catch in my throat as I take in the scene behind me.

Jace, in all his steel-cut, handsome glory, is stalking toward me through the crowd.

Chapter Ten

"Jace," I whisper, my veins heating with the look he sends my way. In a second, he's in front of me, crushing his mouth to mine with a hunger I've never felt before.

"You look absolutely stunning, sunshine," he growls, his cock twitching against my hip. Twisting me around, he hugs me from behind, pressing against my ass with a groan.

"Do you think anyone would notice if I fucked you right here?" he muses, his fingertips trailing over the hem at the back of my slinky black dress. His hand pushes between my thighs, moving with excruciating leisure toward my core.

"It would be so... easy," he moans, pressing two fingers inside me.

"Jace!" I yelp, my eyes shifting nervously around the packed bar. "Someone's going to see."

"I sure hope so," he groans, swirling his knuckles against my walls. "You look positively beautiful when you come."

"You okay, Cass?" My head whips to Kasey, heat creeping up my neck at the knowing smirk on her face. "Want me to grab you some water?"

"I'm f-fine," I squeak, biting my lip to suppress a moan as Jace presses into my spot.

"You sure? You look a little red." She grins, shooting a look at where Jace's hand rests between my legs. "I think the bathroom is empty."

With a growl, Jace removes his hand and throws me over his shoulder. I let out a shriek, but Jace doesn't seem to notice as he storms toward the bathroom stalls.

"Hey, Jace!" a man's voice says to our left, but I can't see his face from behind Jace's burly shoulder. "You got a sec? I need to talk to you about—"

"Not now!" Jace hisses. I almost feel bad for the guy, but then Jace grips my ass possessively, and the thought flies out the window. Kicking open the door to the bathroom, he does a scan of the stalls to make sure we're alone before placing me on the ground.

"On your knees. Now," Jace orders. The lock clicks as my knees hit the tile, and the next second, Jace is in front of me, ripping his thick leather belt from his waist.

"Open," he orders with a pointed look at my mouth. My lips part, and Jace pushes two fingers into my mouth.

"Suck." My tongue swirls his digits, and a salty taste coats my mouth. "Do you like how you taste?" He grins, pulling his fingers away and placing them in his own mouth. He moans, his pupils blowing as he sucks the rest of me from his hand. "Fucking addicting."

My core throbs as he pulls his cock out, my mouth already watering with the need to taste him. He presses the tip against my lips, spreading the pre cum along my lower lip.

"Are you going to be a good girl and suck my cock?" he asks, his voice choked with desire. I nod, spreading my lips as wide as they'll go to accommodate his size.

His cock hits the back of my throat, and tears spring to my eyes as I try in vain to choke him down. Even with all my efforts, he only makes it halfway in, and I quickly bring my hand up to stroke the rest of his length while I swirl my tongue around the head.

"Oh fuck, Cassandra," he moans, fisting his fingers in the back of my hair. "That's so good. Just like that, dirty girl."

Pride swells in my chest as I take him deeper, fighting the need to spit out the massive foreign object in my throat. His cock swells, throbs, and I know he's close to exploding.

"Fuck. Not yet," he growls, tearing his cock from my mouth. Drool pools from my mouth and down my neck, but Jace doesn't give me time to recover, and he fits his hands under my arms and hauls me from the floor.

Without asking, he spins me around so my ass presses against his cock, his fists tightening around my hips and keeping me locked in place. Wrapping one arm around my belly, he uses the other to hike my dress over my ass. Jace moans low in his throat as he fists my panties and rips them from my body.

"From now on, you will not wear panties when I see you. Understood?"

I nod, not wanting to mention that I wasn't planning to see him tonight. His palm connects with my ass, and I yelp, heat creeping up my spine from the affected area.

"Words, dirty girl."

"Yes, sir," I murmur, my face heating. "I understand."

"Good. I need access to you at all times. Because this..." His hand creeps toward my clit. "Is fucking addicting."

The head of his cock teases my entrance for barely a second before he slams inside me. I cry out, my eyes watering as I try desperately to acclimate to his size.

"Always so fucking wet for me," he moans, slamming in and out of me mercilessly. "Such a good little dirty girl."

The fullness paired with the relentless teasing of my clit makes me soar. Light sparks behind my lids as I come, every nerve in my body firing with such intense pleasure it makes my knees crumple.

"Jace!" My ears are deaf to the scream that pours from my lips as my walls shudder around his cock.

"Fuck, yes!" Jace groans, his cock throbbing inside me, filling me with hot ropes of cum. He moves slowly now, drawing out every last shudder of my pleasure, pushing his seed deeper inside me. With a growl, his cock slips out of me, and he holds me even tighter to him while placing tender kisses along my spine.

"You did so good, dirty girl," he mutters, sinking his teeth into my shoulder. I gasp, a spark of pain shooting from the area that fades into a dull ache of pleasure. "You take my cock so fucking well. I'll never get enough of this pussy. Never get enough of *you*."

I turn to give him a kiss, and a pounding noise makes its way through the door.

"Hey! Open up!"

Jace actually *growls*, his eyes shooting fire where

the person would be standing. "Just a minute!" he shouts, letting go of my hips so he can put his pants back in place. "You okay, sunshine?"

"Yeah," I murmur, pulling my dress back over my ass. "Just a little embarrassed."

Jace chuckles low in his throat. "That's okay. You'll get used to it after a few times."

"A few... times?" My eyes widen. I assumed Jace was kinky, but I didn't know he was a do-it-in-public kinda guy.

He nods, his dimples popping with an earth shattering smirk. "There's so many things I want to show you, dirty girl. So many different ways to pleasure you."

My throat bobs as Jace snakes his hand around my waist. Something about the promise makes my knees weak, and I have a feeling it won't be long until we put his ideas into practice.

Leading me to the door, he twists the lock and throws it open, refusing to spare the seething woman on the other side a single glance.

"Hey, asshole!"

"That's Mr. Asshole, to you." Jace throws a glare over his shoulder. "And unless you want to be thrown out, I suggest you shut up and do your business. You seemed *very* impatient, earlier."

Without another word, Jace turns and leads me

across the dance floor. It takes me a moment to figure out where we're headed, and then I see Kasey making out with some Greek god in the corner.

When she comes up for air, Jace taps her on the shoulder, and she swivels to face us. "Cass! I want you to meet Marvin!" she squeals, her words slightly slurred. "Isn't he gorgeous?" Palming both sides of Marvin's face, she physically turns him side to side so we can get a look.

When she finally lets go, he gives us a helpless look. "That's not actually my name. I've been trying all night to tell her that it's really F—"

"Hush, Marvin!" Kasey pushes her finger to his lips, cutting him off. "You're prettier when you don't speak."

I mouth an apology to Not-Marvin, grabbing Kasey by the arm so her attention is back on me. "I think it's time to head home, hun."

"Wha-nooo!" she cries, throwing her arms out. She narrowly misses the side of Not-Marvin's face, and I step forward, pushing them back to her sides.

"Yes." I give Jace a nod over my shoulder. He steps forward, throwing Kasey over his shoulder before I have time to blink.

"Stop this!" she shouts, beating her fists on his shoulder. "I do *not* like being handled, buddy! I don't care if my best friend is madly in love with you. I'll kick you right in the gonads!"

Jace turns to me, a worried look creasing his forehead. "Did she just say gonads?"

"Afraid so." I sigh, holding open the door for him. He ducks under the frame, and we make our way to the car with Kasey blubbering in the background. "She gets a little dramatic when she's had five too many."

Jace shrugs, tipping his chin for me to open the car door. He places her on the seat and backs away, letting me buckle her in. "I'm just glad I was here to help you get her out of there. I'm not sure how you do it on your own."

"Lots and lots of coaxing." I sigh, stepping back and shutting the door. Jace pulls me into his chest, his steady heartbeat a reminder that he'll be my rock, no matter what. I'm starting to come to terms with the fact I don't have to do it all alone, and I've never felt more at peace.

"I don't mean to add anything else to your plate, but..." He shakes his head, seeming to think better of it. "You know what? It can wait until the morning."

I pull back, narrowing my eyes. "Well, now you have to tell me. Make it quick, please. The suspense might just kill me."

Jace's chest shakes. "If you insist... Janet's been

emailing me nonstop about you. She wants you to come into the studio and talk to her."

"About what?"

His muscles tense. "I may have let it slip that you just quit your job. I think she wants to offer you a position at the studio."

I choke on whatever I thought I was going to say. Surely, he means some menial position, like sharpening the pencils or cleaning up after class. But then again... what if it's something more? Could I handle the rejection if I get my hopes up and it isn't?

"I don't know," I mutter, fisting my hand around my golden sun. "I don't think it's such a good idea."

"Why not?" Jace looks genuinely confused. "This is a chance to make a living doing something you love, Cass. You don't even want to hear what she has to say?"

"Maybe... I don't know." I sigh. "I just recently came to terms with the accident and what it's left me with. If I try again... If I fail... I don't know who I'll be then. If there will be anything left to put back together."

Jace face crumples, and for a while, he's silent. His arms tighten around my shoulders, and it feels like he's trying to pull all my pain into his body, to take away the doubts and feelings of utter inadequacy.

"I'll be here this time. If you can't do it yourself, I'll

hold you until you're whole. You don't have to do it alone anymore. I'm here now, sunshine. I'm here."

My shoulders shake as I cry silently into his chest, letting out all the fear and pain I've been holding inside for this past year. He's right. I'm not alone. I don't think I ever will be again.

"Let's get you home," he murmurs, pressing his lips to the top of my head. "We'll drop Kasey off at her place, and I'll run you a bubble bath. Pop a bottle of red and get you nice and relaxed for your interview tomorrow. How's that sound?"

"Tomorrow?" I squeak, hoping I heard him wrong. "When did that get decided?"

"Since I told Janet you'd be there. Come on, sunshine. Sometimes it's like you think I don't know you." He gives me that devastating smirk, and my fingers go numb. "Hop in. We gotta make sure you get at least a little sleep tonight."

Chapter Eleven

I STARE AT THE ROW OF BOXY OFFICE buildings and will my feet to move in the direction of the doors. A sharp twinge of pain shoots through my bad wrist as doubt begins to fill my gut, and I debate whether to just leave this place before I embarrass myself even more than I have.

"I'll be waiting here for you. Go get 'em." Jace winks, pressing his lips to the side of my temple. "We already know she wants you to work there. There's no need for you to be nervous."

I shake my head, reminding myself that he's right. In any case, it would be rude to cancel at the last minute on the woman nice enough to look past my artistic flaws. With one last kiss from Jace, I stride toward the clear glass doorway and into the art building.

I make my way up the stairs to the main studio the same way Kasey and I had all those nights ago, my knees shaking with each step. I rap my knuckles lightly on the closed wooden door, and barely a moment later, I'm greeted by Janet's smiling eyes.

"Hello! Come in, come in!" She grins warmly and opens the door wider for easy passage. "Please excuse the mess. I tried to get the room straightened up before you got here but, well... You can see how well that went." She chuckles.

"It's no problem at all," I say, my mouth lifting into its own satisfied little smile at the sight of a well-used studio. "I'm pretty messy when I work too." My face heats with the realization that I may have just offended her.

Instead, Janet arches her head in a laugh. "The best artists are, you know." She winks easily at me. "Just between the two of us."

If possible, my face reddens to an even darker shade as she leads me over to a set of metal folding chairs.

"So, um... Jace told me you wanted to talk to me about a job?" My words are more of a question than a statement.

"Desperately." She huffs as she plops in one of the seats. "I mean, seriously, at this point, I'm willing to give away a kidney to anyone who wants to help me deal with this." She gestures around the room.

"And you just need help with general cleaning and organizing for the most part, right?"

Janet cocks her head at me with a question swirling in her eyes. "Is that all you *want* to do?"

"Well, not really, but..."

Her head does a little shake of amusement. "I had something else in mind. I was hoping you'd teach a few classes a week? You know, give me a night off every now and again." She gives me that knowing wink again.

At her suggestion, another sharp pain runs the length of my wrist like a reminder, and I find myself at a loss for words.

"You'll obviously be paid the full instructor's salary if you decide to do that, of course," Janet adds, clearly taking my silence as worry about the matter of money. I almost feel bad that I have to tell her the truth.

"Listen, I really, *really* appreciate you offering, but..." I reach my good hand over to massage my throbbing wrist. "I don't really think I'm qualified for that kind of position."

"What? Nonsense!" Janet shakes her head aggressively as if trying to convince herself she heard wrong. "I've seen your work. If anything, I'd say you were *over*qualified for this job."

I open my mouth to protest, but before I get a word out, she continues with her convincing act.

"You can even use the studio space in your free time! All the paint, canvases, and supplies are at your disposal. A starving artist's wet dream, if you ask me!"

I try to lift my mouth into a smile but find the effort too great. If only she knew how far I actually was from what she described me as, and how much it hurt to admit I never would be again.

"Look, the issue isn't any of those things... it's that I physically *can't.*" My voice is hoarse as I hold my scarred wrist to the light. "I was in a surfing accident a while ago. Almost lost my entire hand, but the surgeon on call that day was supposedly some medical genius and was able to save it." I take a deep breath to steady my voice before continuing. "I've been to at least twenty different physical therapists and doctors... but even the best-case scenario leaves me with only fifty percent of my original mobility. I really don't want you to think I'm being ungrateful," I whisper, my eyes focused on my hands clasped tightly in my lap. "But I just think I'd be embarrassing myself and everyone else if I tried to actually teach a class."

I finally raise my eyes to meet hers, expecting some form of sympathy to be splayed across her face like with all the others I've told. Instead, there's a hardened glint that shakes me to my core.

"Have you noticed anything strange about my face,

Cassandra?" she asks, looking at me straight on. "Maybe about my eyes?"

"Well, no, not real—" I stop as soon as I notice something about her right eye. You can't tell unless you're specifically looking, but now that she mentions it, one of her eyes *is* slightly more dull than the other. In fact, it almost looks... plastic.

Without thinking, my mouth pops open in surprise. "Your eye... It's... Is it fake?"

Janet nods, the stony expression from earlier replaced with the kind, joyful one I'm accustomed to. "That's right. Lost it and about half of the vision in the other when I was about your age, actually."

She sighs tiredly. "I was jumping off the rocks in the cove with a bunch of my friends one day, except when it was my turn to jump, I lost my footing and went headfirst to the rocks below. The optic nerve in my left eye was damaged when I hit my head, and the right was lost to trauma.

"Honestly, it's a wonder I survived at all," she says. "But though it hurts me to admit, for a while I remember wishing that I hadn't. You see, like you, I was talented. I had my whole future ahead of me, and it was looking so stinking bright. With my depth perception went my dreams of furthering my career. For a while, I convinced myself I would never paint again. I couldn't deal with the heartache that came with struggling days and weeks over a piece that used to take me a couple of hours to knock out. Not to mention that each new one continued to look worse than the last, even with all that extra time spent."

Janet looks off to the side, her eyes misty and red from the memory. "I'm telling you this because I *know* what it's like to lose the thing that makes you, you. To deal with the pain and knowledge every day that you might not ever be as good as you once were. But Cassandra." She pauses for a moment to look into my eyes, her tone adamant as she tells me, "*Fuck* what those doctors told you. Matter of fact, fuck anyone who has ever put any doubt in your mind about this. Just because something horrible happened to you doesn't mean you have to give up the things you love most."

I wring my hands in my lap until my knuckles go white, listening patiently as my chest tightens with the first sprinkle of hope I've allowed myself to feel in over a year.

I drag my eyes back to hers, not even slightly embarrassed that my own tears are threatening to break free. "You... do you really think that I can do it? That one day I can draw like I used to?"

The corner of Janet's eyes crinkles with a motherly smile as she rests a paint-speckled hand on top of mine.

"You don't need to take my word for it. How's about seeing for yourself?"

I leave shortly after accepting the position. Janet practically jumped out of her seat in excitement when I finally caved and told her I would try. And though I'm not ready to admit it to myself, I'm actually excited for my first day of teaching an actual art class.

Jace waits on the sidewalk where I left him, a knowing grin lighting his handsome face. The way his eyes roam over my body sets fire to my belly, and I nearly trip on the last step.

"Shit! You okay?" I don't know how he got to me so fast, but his hands are on my shoulders, steadying me while my knees continue their furious quaking.

"I'm... more than okay." My face feels like it will split in half as I beam at him. "She wants me to teach a class."

"I know." He presses a kiss on the tip of my nose. "Janet told me that, too."

"You jerk!" I swat him playfully. "Why didn't you tell me? I was literally freaking out this entire morning."

Jace gives me a pointed look. "If *I* was the one to tell you, you wouldn't have believed it. Or worse, convinced yourself it was some elaborate prank and canceled at the last second."

My cheeks heat, knowing I don't have a quip for that. *Damn him. I hate how well he knows me sometimes.*

"You ready to celebrate?" he asks, scooping me in his arms and stalking to his car.

"I think so," I whisper, losing my mind with his strong arms tightening around me. He places me in the passenger seat, securing my buckle and placing a kiss on my cheek.

"Precious cargo: secured." He grins, pulling back to close the door. Sliding in his seat, he shifts gears and peels down the road, resting his hand comfortably on my thigh as the scenery whips past us.

We drive in silence for a few minutes, the gentle rumble of the asphalt beneath the tires lulling me into a haze. That is, until Jace's hand slides toward my core. His fingertips slip past the hem of my shorts, teasing my clit with a whisper of a touch.

A mewl pours from my lips, and I subconsciously shift so he has better access. A smirk lights Jace's face at the sound, and his movements become more intentional, swirling and pressing the sensitive nub.

"Jace," I hiss, but it comes out more like a desperate moan. "You need to stop that."

"Stop what?" His voice lilts innocently as he slips his index in to join the other finger.

"*That,*" I groan, arching my head back open-mouthed as he massages me, dipping the tips of his fingers past my wetness and pumping gently.

"You don't really seem like you want me to." Jace turns toward me with a knowing grin, his pupils blown and making his eyes appear black. "Or am I wrong?"

I'm lost for words as his fingers start playing with my clit, so I let out a deep moan that should be answer enough. He continues toying with me, his touch relentless and controlled as he brings me closer and closer to the edge.

"Oh fuck yes, right there." I pant, wriggling my body against the seat. "Please, God, don't stop."

"Good girl," Jace coos, his voice hoarse with desire. "Now come for your god."

With one last, gentle swirl of his index, I explode in his hand, keeling my head back in the seat as the orgasm tears through my system. Stars spark in the backs of my eyes as I ride out wave after wave of pleasure, unable to think of anything but Jace's fingers inside me.

"Fuck," Jace breathes, slipping his hand out and bringing it to his mouth to suck my wetness off his fingers. "I think I'm addicted to the way you taste."

"I think you should watch the road," I murmur, my face heated from both embarrassment and the intensity of my climax. His touch is like a drug to my system, and no matter how many times I had him, he still managed to give me a better high than the last.

Jace lets out a chuckle from deep in his chest. "I just made you come, and you *still* have the energy to give me sass, huh?"

"Till the day I die." I grin contentedly as I snuggle deeper into the seat, watching from the corner of my eye as Jace attempts to readjust.

"Don't give me that little smirk," Jace growls, sending me a quick warning glance. "Just because I'm driving doesn't mean I won't pull over and throw you over my knee."

"First he's sweet, then he's sour." I giggle as the muscle in Jace's jaw ticks.

"Oh, you're so in for it," Jace rumbles, unable to stop the smile from entering his voice. "Just wait till I get you home."

"I honestly don't know if I can," I quip, shooting him a cheesy wink. He stays silent for a while, the tension building in the cabin until it feels like I'll choke on it.

"Penny for your thoughts?" I tuck my legs and turn in the seat, facing him head-on. "They look like they hurt." A dark laugh falls from his lips, and it takes everything in me to hold back a shudder.

"I was just thinking how you've never fucked in a car. It's a rite of passage, you know."

"And here I was, thinking that's what we just did." Fuck, I hope he can't tell how nervous I am.

"I *finger* fucked you, dirty girl. It's not the same thing." He pulls the wheel to the side, parking the car between two massive oaks off the main road. "Plus, there's something I've always wanted to try. Take off your shorts. Now."

The look in his eye causes the hair on the back of my neck to prick, and I don't dare disobey. It takes me a bit longer to get them past my hips in the confined space, but I manage to get them off without looking like too much of a clutz.

He slides as far to the door as possible, leaving about four inches of space on the seat. "Turn around and straddle the dash. That's it, good girl," he coos, gripping my arm to steady me as I get into position. The top of my head hits the ceiling, and I wince, thinking Jace is going to laugh at my clumsiness. When I turn to look, his expression is void of amusement, but there is a spark of something I haven't seen before. Something animalistic. Something dark.

My legs are barely long enough to span the distance between seats, and when I finally get into the position he wants, something round and hard brushes my bare pussy. I blush, knowing I'm practically dripping all over his fancy leather.

Before I have time to voice this, Jace places one palm on my lower back and slides the other down my abdomen, resting at the spot just above my core. With a shudder, he pushes me back and down on that hard thing, his chest heaving with each labored breath. An image of the strangely shaped gear shift enters my mind and I think back to when I first saw it. How I remarked it looked more like a dildo than what it actually was.

With a gasp, I realize what he wants me to do. He wants to fuck me with the gear shift.

"Jace! Fuck!" I cry, digging my fingers into the seats as the head of the gear shift pushes past my tight barrier. "What are you doing?"

"God, you're so fucking wet, it's just sliding right in," he whispers, his pupils blowing as he pushes me farther down. "You're such a good girl, Cassandra. Such a dirty fucking girl. Just look at you, taking a goddamn shift in your cunt."

His hands cup my shoulders, using the added momentum to push the last inch inside me. I cry out, tears welling in my eyes from being split in two.

"My fucking God," Jace whispers, taking in the sight with hungry eyes. "What's wrong, dirty girl?

Don't you want to give me any more of that sass?" His grin widens at the same time my eyes do.

"I'll take that as a no." The pressure loosens on my shoulders, and the next second he's gripping my waist, hauling me off the gear shift. The expression on his face paired with the friction is too much, and my orgasm tears through me. A clear fluid shoots across Jace's dash, but I don't have time to be embarrassed about it before he pushes his cock inside me.

"Fuck, I'll never get enough of this pussy," he groans, holding my ass with his palms while he thrusts into me from below. My head falls back as he slams deeper, harder, and I scream, not giving a fuck if anyone can hear us out there.

"Yes! Jace, I'm gonna come," I mewl, collapsing forward on his chest as he sinks his teeth into my shoulder.

"Me too, dirty girl," Jace chokes, his jaw ticking furiously. "Fucking come with me."

A scream tears from my throat as my walls collapse, vaguely aware of Jace's cock throbbing somewhere deep inside me. My entire body shudders in the aftermath, barely registering Jace's lips peppering kisses over my shoulder. A groan tumbles from his lips as his cock slips out of me, and he shifts my weight in his arms so I'm more comfortable.

"I love you, Cassandra."

My muscles tense at the words. *Did he just say...*

"That I love you? Yeah, I did," he murmurs, brushing his hand over my hair. "Feels good to finally get it out in the open."

I look up, my lips twitching at the mischievous twinkle in his eyes. "You've been holding this back for a while?"

"You don't even know," he whispers, the vein at the side of his neck thrumming violently. "I don't even care if you don't feel the same way. I just wanted to finally have the chance to tell you. Because I do, Cassandra. Irrevocably. Undeniably. I love you."

"Well, you're in luck." I grin, kissing the tip of his nose. "Because I love you too. Impossibly. Endlessly. I'm so in love with you, it hurts. I think some part of me always has."

The look on his face causes tears to well in my eyes. I would give up all my dreams in a heartbeat to make him smile like that every day. If anyone in this shitty world deserves it, it's Jace Maddox.

"I can't believe you're finally mine," he whispers, brushing his thumb over my cheek like he's checking if I'm real. His cock twitches under me, and my face heats as he chuckles.

"I think it's time to get you home. I need you at least three more times tonight, and I don't plan to do that in the car."

"Yes, sir." I giggle, sliding back into the passenger seat and shoving my tongue at him.

"Watch it," he growls, his voice shaking with a laugh. "And put your seat belt on."

"*Yes, sir.*"

Chapter Twelve

A YAWN TEARS FROM MY MOUTH, SO SUDDEN and powerful that the charcoal pencil slips from my palm. Exhaustion fuzzing the edges of my vision, I get on all fours and search for the tool. I've worn all my other pencils to nubs, so if I want to get any more work done today, I really need to find the damn thing.

"If I were a lousy piece of charcoal, where would I hide?" I wonder, trying to ignore the dull throb between my thighs. I'm not sure if it was what happened in the car, but Jace couldn't keep his hands off me last night. Or his cock out of me, to be more accurate.

"Screw this," I grumble, unable to push through the ache any longer. Hobbling back to my stool, I plop with a heavy sigh. *Sitting has never felt so good.* My chin hits my chest, and I'm about to shut my eyes when I see a flash of something black behind the foot of my easel.

"You little asshole." I narrow my eyes as I lean down, pinching the pencil between my fingers. *Guess that's a sign I need to get some more work done, after all.*

I take a moment to stretch out the stiffness in my joints before positioning the charcoal tip in my dominant hand. It's a bit awkward, considering my lack of flexibility, but I've found ways to work around it.

My lungs fill with a breath, and I press the tip to the canvas, shutting off my brain and letting the medium guide me. I still deal with the fear that it might turn out horribly, that something I put my heart and soul into will be laughed out of the room. It's crippling, but I'm trying my best to push through it so I can be proud of myself someday.

"Oh my word, Cass. It looks incredible."

I startle at Janet's voice, knocking the tip of my nose against the canvas. I hadn't even realized how focused I'd been or how close I've gotten to the piece while detailing.

"Sorry, dear, I didn't mean to scare you." Janet chuckles and rests a hand on my shoulder as she leans in to inspect my art. "I love all the emotion you've managed to add to the eyes. You really do have a knack for that sort of thing."

"Thank you," I whisper, my chest swelling as I

look at the piece. The black and white side profile of some nameless woman stares back at me, her mouth fixed open with her hands cupping her throat as if she's screaming in anguish, but no sound will come, and no one will be able to hear her pain.

"It's not exactly the quality I'm used to, though…" I murmur, taking in each jagged and imperfect edge with a critical eye. "I can't seem to get the hands quite right."

"Nonsense." Janet waves me off. "This is a wonderful representation of emotion in art."

"I'll take your word for it." I sigh, standing from my stool to give my legs and back a much-needed stretch.

"Now just what did we say about taking *my* word?" Janet chuckles. "You'll see for yourself this weekend."

"And you're *positive* I'm ready to teach?" I ask. I'd spent the past week following Janet around the studio and sitting in on all her classes to learn the ropes. And though she's reassured me time and time again that I am more than prepared to start, I still feel more like an impostor than someone qualified to teach others.

"Does a mouse like cheese?" she chirps, giving me that knowing wink of hers as she makes her way over to my pencil nubs. "Need me to replace these for you?"

"That would actually be a blessing," I say, looking

around at the giant mess I've managed to create in the past few hours. "I still have to clean all this other junk before I head out for the evening."

"Oh, don't worry about that." Janet wrinkles her nose at the thought of cleaning. "Just make sure all of the tables are wiped down. The rest can get taken care of tomorrow."

"Sounds good to me." I give her a bright smile as she makes her way out of the studio, elated that I won't have to be here for another hour, making sure everything is spotless.

I start going around my station, closing all the supplies I had used, when the door cracks open again.

"Forget something again?" I chuckle, not even bothering to turn back from what I was doing. Usually, when she has to come back into the room, she makes a big deal about how she's losing her marbles like her mother.

"Everything okay?" I call over my shoulder when Janet doesn't say anything. Still nothing.

Confused, I whip around, and my heart leaps. Jace leans against the doorframe, his crisp gray suit straining deliciously over his chest and biceps. His dimples pop as he shoves off the frame, stalking toward me with a starved look in his eyes.

"I thought you had a meeting," I whisper.

"Canceled." He stops just in front of me, his jaw ticking. "I couldn't keep away."

My thighs pulse with a reminder of how much he's used me already, and I give him a sheepish grin. "I'm kind of sore..."

"Good," he growls, scooping me up and stomping to one of the work desks. Holding me to him with one arm, he swipes the other across the top, scattering various art supplies across the floor. My ass hits the wood, and I barely have time to blink before Jace strips me of my shorts.

"What did I fucking tell you about these?" he hisses, fisting the base of my silk panties. A tearing sound fills the space, and the next thing I know, the remnants are balled in his fist.

His dark eyes glint menacingly as he leans in. "I guess I'll just have to show you what happens when you disobey me." My mouth pops, and Jace uses the opportunity to shove my used panties inside. I choke, my tongue fighting against the cloth creeping to the back of my throat.

"You want to be my dirty girl, don't you?" he coos, taking two fingers and pushing them farther inside. Tears prick my eyes, and I nod, trying to take quick, shallow breaths.

"Then stop fucking fighting and let me teach you your lesson," he growls, undoing his belt with his free hand. The head of his cock teases my entrance, and a garbled moan pushes past the barrier filling my mouth.

"Your pussy is crying for me, dirty girl. You might think you're sore, but I don't think she got the fucking message." He eases his length inside, and my eyes roll back, loving the way his cock fills every last inch of me.

"Fuck, yes," he groans, thrusting with more power. The table bangs against the wall with a violent rhythm, but I don't even care if someone hears or someone sees. All I want is for Jace to give me that earth-shattering release that I only seem to find on his cock.

"Fuck me, dirty girl. You're gonna make me come," he groans, slowing his thrusts in an attempt to delay the inevitable.

I shake my head violently, hooking my ankles around his waist and pulling him deep inside me. When his head hits the back of my walls, I come undone. My head falls back as I convulse around him, and shortly after, he throbs with his own release.

"Fuck me," he hisses, pumping the last of his seed deep inside before slipping out. "God, I love the way you look with my cum dripping out of you."

With my senses returning, so does my embarrassment. The back of my neck heats as it pools beneath me, and I squirm in his grip. With a hungry look, he pulls the panties from my mouth and shoves them into his jacket pocket.

"Jace, someone could walk in, and—"

"You mean someone like me?" Janet's lilt sends white-hot shame straight to my marrow, and I instinctually shove my face into Jace's chest. With his back to her, Jace zips his cock back into his slacks, his whole body shaking with a chuckle.

"Sorry about that, Janet." He smirks over his shoulder at her. "Couldn't help myself."

"Don't say sorry to me." She huffs. "You better apologize to all the art supplies you ruined." Her voice is meant to be stern, but I can't help but notice the thread of amusement weaved in.

"You'll be getting a check for it. Scout's honor," he says, crouching and feeding my legs through the holes of my shorts.

"I can do that," I mutter, knowing my face is at least twenty different shades of mortification.

"I know. I just like taking care of you." He smirks, the look on his face telling me it's pointless to argue. As soon as the button is in place, I hop down from the table, standing strategically in front of the giant wet spot. I can't look Janet in the eye, so I opt to stare at her velvet ballet flats.

A laugh titters through the air. "Oh, sweetie. I'd be lying if I hadn't done the same thing. Not a day goes by that I don't think about Rafael..." She gives her head a little shake before continuing. "You know, some of the best art pieces are inspired by sex." She gives me a wink, and I will the ground to swallow me whole.

Jace lets loose a full-bellied laugh, finding far more amusement with the situation than me. "We'll make sure to clean before we head out. And I'll get that check to you before I leave." His arm wraps around me, and he pulls me tight against his side.

Janet's eyes trail to the table, taking in the large discoloration of the wood. "I would suggest bleach... you two have fun." She grins, placing the sharpened pencils on one of the other tables before swirling out of the room. "I'll see you later, Cassandra!"

"See you later," I mutter, hiding my face in Jace's suit. *I cannot believe that just happened. Fuck my life.*

Jace presses his lips to the top of my head. "Well, I guess we better get to it. We gotta get out of here before the sun sets."

"Why?" My brows come together. "What happens at sunset?"

Jace shrugs, a cryptic smile on his face. "The sharks come out."

Chapter Thirteen

JACE'S HAND RESTS COMFORTABLY ON MY thigh as he steers down Main Street. I glance at the silver gear shift, my cheeks heating at the memory of what it was used for.

"Are we almost there?" At my line of questioning, his palm contracts, and he gives the area a rough squeeze.

"You really need to learn how to enjoy the journey, sunshine." He grins, shooting me a glance out of the corner of his eye. "Just trust me when I tell you that you'll love it."

I huff and cross my arms over my chest in a pout so dramatic, it would have put a toddler to shame.

"Well, then could you tell me what's under that damn tarp in the back? It's giving 'serial killer' vibes, and I'm not really in the mood to be unalived today."

With a scoff, Jace shakes his head. "Not a chance. Especially not after that comment. You'll just have to be a little more patient."

"I think you just like watching me suffer," I grumble. "Ya damn sadist, you."

Jace's fingertips dig into my thigh as he barks a laugh. "If I'm a sadist, that makes you the biggest masochist in the world."

"That title is just so restrictive. I prefer sadist abler."

"Whatever helps you sleep at night." He turns to give me that heartbreaking grin of his, and I'm suddenly very grateful to be sitting down.

"You're gonna give me a heart attack one of these days," I mutter.

"What was that?"

"I said you're going to give me an ulcer with all these secrets," I grumble, scrunching further into the seat as Jace has a good laugh at my expense.

"Just relax, would you? Have I ever taken you somewhere you hated?"

"Not to my knowledge... but there's always a first," I remind him.

I can practically feel the eye roll in his voice as he tells me, "If you really end up hating it that much, I'll find something else to make it up to you. How's that sound?"

"Much better." I grin, uncrossing my arms and sitting straight again. "And that something better involve ice cream, just so you know."

"Whatever you want, sunshine," Jace agrees. "You could ask for the moon, and I'd find some way to get it down here for you."

"No way. Think of what that would do to the tide. Absolute hell would be wreaked on the sea turtles." I shake my head in mock disappointment, "And you call yourself an animal lover."

Jace rolls his eyes. "Let a man try to be romantic every now and again, would you?"

I proceed to fall into a fit of giggles as Jace whips the wheel of the car to the right down another side street. As I glance out the window, I suddenly realize where we are—and, even more alarming—where we're headed.

"Jace," my voice comes out hollow. "Why are we driving in the direction of the beach?"

At my question, he remains uncharacteristically silent and continues down the road.

"Jace?" I ask again, my voice beginning to rise in hysteria.

"Cass, it's okay." He gives my thigh another reassuring squeeze. "I know you're scared, but I think this will be really good for you."

"Wha—good for me *how?*"

"Because you love surfing, Cass," Jace deadpans, pulling his eyes from the road to give me a look that makes my protest die in my throat. "Your accident didn't change that, and I don't think anything ever will. It's a part of you, just like art is. And I'll be damned if I sit here and let you stop yourself from doing the things you love out of fear."

"But I—"

"Cassandra Stone," Jace barks, effectively cutting me off. "Are you really going to let fear rule your life? Are you going to lie down and let it fuck you in the ass and say thank you? Or are you going to stand up, puff out your chest, and scream *fuck you* to fear?"

"Well, I certainly don't want anything to do with the former," I murmur, trying to hold back the laughter rising in my chest.

"Dear God, woman," Jace groans, shaking his head side to side with a small smile playing on his lips. "If anyone in this car will end up with an ulcer, it's definitely me."

"What? You're the one giving me shitty scenarios to choose from! What else was I supposed to say?"

"Honestly? I was hoping you would scream 'fuck you, fear' while pumping your fist in the air like in those shitty kids cartoons."

"I'm not sure what shows *you* were watching growing up, but for us cultured folk, the f-word is kind of a big no-no." I giggle as he shoots me a fed-up look out of the corner of his eye.

"Well, looks like you're gonna have to act grown and say it because we're here."

The truck slows as Jace pulls into a secluded parking area next to the beach access point, and whatever confidence I had earlier vanishes. Jace leaves the key in the ignition as he turns to me, giving my thigh a reassuring squeeze before cupping my chin in his palm.

"I want you to know I would never force you to do anything. I know you're scared, but I promise that if you decide not to go now, you'll regret it for the rest of your life." His dark brows knit together in a deep frown as he whispers, "I can't let you live with that regret. So please, Cass, will you trust me?"

With one glance at the look on his face, I know my answer immediately. I pull the lever to the door and hop out onto the ground as fast as my shaking knees will let me.

"Come on, slowpoke." I grin at him with all the confidence I wish I had. "Last one to the shore has to give the other a back massage tonight."

Jace's face morphs from one of concern to pride in a matter of milliseconds. With a broad smile that certainly didn't help the state of my knees, he follows suit and slides out of the driver's seat.

"I certainly hope you're ready to dish out the

prizes." Jace grins, and with that, we peel off toward the ocean.

"Why did I let you talk me into this?" The cry that tears from my throat is half hysterical, half genuine terror. A massive unbroken wave is heading straight for me, threatening to suck me into the endless swell.

Turning my board's nose directly in line with the oncoming wave, I tuck my chin into my chest and hold my body flush against the board. With one last gulp of air, I plunge the tip into the wave and let it pass through me, continuing its path toward the shore. When I finally surface at the other end, I have to spend at least five minutes coughing up all the saltwater in my lungs.

"This is literally the worst," I grumble, loosening my death grip on the surfboard. "Literally. How did I ever think this was fun?"

It's been over half an hour, and I still haven't even attempted to head out into deeper waters. The last wave wasn't much bigger than the whitewater beginner's ride, but heading toward me, it felt like a monsoon. I'm clearly not brave enough to face this fear.

"You know, if you drink all the salt water, there won't be any left for the fish!" Jace's teasing lilt rings out across the water.

"Thanks, I'll be sure to keep that in mind," I grumble, watching as he effortlessly glides toward me through the tide. His wetsuit clings to his frame like a second skin, and for a moment, I forget how terrified I am as I watch his muscles ripple with each powerful stroke.

"Why don't we try heading out a little deeper? Give you something to challenge you a little?" he asks, grinning at me with those damn dimples. They could make me agree to anything.

"Did you not see what happened? I don't think a 'challenge' is what I need right now."

Jace shakes his head like *I'm* the one being ridiculous. "You're overthinking everything. What you need to do is stop thinking and let your instincts take over."

"What, so I can end up as fish food when a big daddy wave takes me out? Thanks, but no thanks." I huff, sticking my chin in the air so he knows I mean business.

Jace barks a laugh. "Big daddy wave? Did you really just say that?"

"You bet your sexy ass." I giggle. "Wait. Don't you make me laugh! You're trying to distract me so I end up going deeper!" I cry, pointing an accusatory finger his way.

"That's what she said."

"Ugh! Stop it! I don't wanna." I push my bottom lip out toward him.

"Do you want some incentive?"

"Oh!" That piques my interest. "Are we talking other than the massage? Because I totally beat you earlier."

"That's only because I was carrying *both* boards." Jace rolls his eyes playfully. "If you had carried your weight, I would totally be cashing in."

"Says the man who physically *took* the board from my arms!"

"Well, what else was I supposed to do? You were gonna stab someone's eye out if I let you carry on like that."

"Oh, whatever," I mutter, though I can't help the small smile tugging at my lips.

Jace cups a hand into the water to splash me. "Go on. Get. Show me what a badass you are."

"What happened to the incentive?"

"This is it." He smirks, showering me with a mighty splash of seawater.

"Fucking dimples," I grumble, wiping the water from my eyes as I turn my board away from the shore.

Balancing on the sweet spot of my board so the nose sticks out of the water, I splay my legs straight behind me and let the tops of my feet dip into the water for stability, then start a steady forward stroke toward deeper water. My shoulders burn from the effort, but I push the pain from my mind and keep paddling with a sense of determination I haven't felt in over a year.

A few moments later, I stop where I am and rest my arms on my board, a sixth sense coming back to me after so many months out of the water.

There she is. My face breaks into a giant grin. It doesn't look like much in the distance, but my experience tells me it'll be one of the day's biggest waves. Now, all I have to do is sit and be patient.

My grin falters. *Will I really be able to do it?* I turn my head back to the side, my eyes searching desperately for the handsome, smiling face.

Sensing my hesitation, Jace calls out over the distance, "You got this, sunshine! Ride that wave better than you do me!"

A giggle bursts from my mouth despite all my nerves, and I give him a big thumbs-up. If nothing else, the man can always replace my nervous butterflies with the good kind.

I turn my attention back to the wave, my eyes widening when I realize how close it's gotten.

"Good goobly gob," I mutter. "I don't remember them being that fast."

My nerves start to falter, but I raise my chin in defiance at the tsunami heading my way. If she wants a fight, I'm going to give her one.

As soon as the wave gains height, I turn my board toward the shore and stroke hard and fast to gain speed in time with the tide. As my body begins to rise, I paddle even harder to the peak of the wave, my face fixed in determination.

Knowing I only have a split second to get this right, I place my hands on either side of my chest and tuck my toes, rising from the board in a cobra-like position. Like a spring, I tuck my legs to my chest and plant them sideways on the board in a low crouch, using my fingertips to balance as I slowly raise my body into a standing position.

My heartbeat slows as I effortlessly catch the face of the wave, riding out the massive surge as it breaks and turns to whitewater inches from my tail. The muscles in my thighs scream from the effort of holding the position, but not nearly as much as my cheeks from the massive smile I can't seem to shake. I can hardly hear Jace's screams of elation over the roar of the water, and my eyes well with tears as I near the shore.

As soon as I make it back onto solid ground, I

throw my board to the side and fall to the sand in a fit of laughter, my legs collapsing beneath me in relief.

"Fuck yes! I knew you could do it!" I turn my head to see Jace running full pelt toward me, ditching his board unceremoniously behind him in the sand as he nears.

My body is knocked backward onto the ground as Jace crashes into me, wrapping his strong arms around my frame and giving me the bear hug of the century.

Nuzzling his face into my neck, he whispers, "I'm so fucking proud of you, Cass. I knew you could do it." He arches back, taking my face in one of his massive palms. "You're absolutely, positively wonderful. So strong, and you don't even realize it," he whispers, his tone reverent.

"And the best part is you're *mine,*" he growls, his eyes darkening with lust as his arms tighten around me. "All. Fucking. Mine."

"*Yours,*" I whisper, loving how his pupils dilate at the simple word. "Always yours."

"Good girl," he growls, lowering his lips onto mine and giving me a soul-shattering kiss. "Now..." He reaches his hand around me to flick the zipper at the back of my wetsuit. "I think it's time we get you out of this and into something a little more... comfy."

I grin at him, my chest rising and falling hard at the insinuation.

"Let's," I agree, laughing as he scoops me off the ground and makes his way back to the truck. I rest my cheek on his chest and allow my eyes to drift close in bliss as he carries me in his arms, feeling—for the first time in a long time—that I can be happy again.

Chapter Fourteen

2 weeks later...

I wipe the back of my palm along my sweat-pricked forehead, leaning back in my stool to give my latest drawing a more critical eye. Spending nearly every day in the studio means my skill has improved quite a bit. Last week, I even finished a piece I didn't hate, which was a big step for me.

The piece I'm working on now? I despise it. The lips are off, and her nostrils look wonky now that I'm farther away from them. And, God, those *hands*. Yuck.

I should just destroy it. Burn it. No one but me should ever lay eyes on this disaster.

I physically shake the negative thoughts away, focusing on the breathing techniques Jace taught me. When I found out he picked it up in a seminar for

CEOs to manage their stress, I scoffed. There's no such thing as *breathing right*, I assured him.

I was wrong.

Closing my eyes, I inhale slowly through my nose, picturing swirls of blue air flowing into my lungs like water into a pitcher. *In and out. In and out.* I press two fingers into my wrist, willing my pulse to return to a steady thrum. Forcing the self-destructive thoughts away.

"It's looking amazing, sunshine."

My eyes fly open, so startled by the voice that I fall backward off my stool.

"Shit!" I screech, flailing my arms and waiting for my skull to meet the ground.

Before I make impact, a familiar pair of arms snake around my shoulders and head, taking the brunt of the force as we topple to the floor.

"Fuck, I'm so sorry." Jace's mouth is curved down as he searches my face for any injury. "Did I hurt you?"

"No, but you're squishing me." I giggle, fisting my fingers in his hair. "I don't mind, though. It's kinda nice." I try to pull his head to mine, but he holds firm.

"As much as I'd like to take you right here and now, we have to get going."

My brows come together. "Going? Going where?" I search my memory to see if we agreed on a date tonight. All my days run together now, and it's not uncommon for him to arrive in a tux and whisk me away to some dinner reservation I've forgotten about.

"I know that look." Jace's dimple pops. "Don't worry, we didn't have plans. I thought I would surprise you since you've been working so hard lately."

"You have, too," I murmur, my eyelids drooping as a familiar warmth spreads to my core. "Why don't we order takeout and spend the night in bed? I'm sure you're just as exhausted as I am."

Jace shakes his head, a mischievous glint in his eyes. "Nope. Not tonight, sunshine. I promise you'll enjoy it, though. Do you trust me?"

"With my life." My smile quickly turns into a frown as Jace pushes off me and stands, holding a hand out to help me up. *Damn. I kinda thought he was bluffing.*

"Fine." I sigh, letting his warm hand engulf mine and pull me from the floor. "But I'm not wearing heels."

Jace steps over to one of the chairs where a silky dress is strewn over the back. He holds it up along with a pair of black Converse, a daring grin on his handsome face.

"I swear, it's like you think I don't know you sometimes."

We drive in comfortable silence for a good half an hour, Jace's calloused palm draped possessively over my bare thigh. It feels like a million degrees in the cabin even though the air is going full blast, and it has everything to do with the tiny circles he makes along my inner thigh.

"Are we almost there?" I whine, shifting in my seat as Jace's index brushes my core. The island is far behind us now, and all I want is for him to pull over and fuck me in the back seat. Hell, he could do it in the trunk, and I'd be happy.

"Look to your right." He jerks his chin out the passenger window while flicking on the turn signal. "You'll know where we are."

A modern building with glass windows making up the walls stands at attention between two huge oak trees. Even from this distance, you can see through the windows and make out the edges of the artwork lining the walls.

"Jace," I breathe, turning to him with a massive smile. "This is awesome. I haven't been to the art gallery in ages."

He squeezes my thigh with a matching grin. "I thought you might enjoy something like this. Especially now that you're getting back into your love of art."

My eye catches a bright red and gold sign at the top

of the stairs leading to the entrance. "Huh. It's up-and-comer night, too. That's cool." My chest sinks with the knowledge that I'll be looking at pieces from artists who actually have a shot at becoming famous. Artists living the dream I once had.

Jace notices the change in my demeanor instantly. "Cass? What happened? We don't have to go if you really don't want to." His tone makes my chest grip with guilt, and I force a smile onto my face.

"No. I want to go. It'll be good for me, really," I promise, though I'm not sure I'm telling either of us the truth.

"Okay. But if you're having a bad time, you tell me. Promise?" he asks, parking the car and turning to me with a worried expression.

"Pinky." I grin, holding the finger out to him. His dimples pop as he hooks his finger in mine, leaning over to kiss the entwined digits. "Let's go, sunshine."

Jace hurries around and opens my door, snaking his hand tightly around my waist and leading me toward the glass doors. Sterile, freezing air-conditioning smacks me in the face as the doors slide open, and goose bumps crawl along my skin. I wish it was from the change in temperature, but I know deep inside it has to do with seeing all the wonderful pieces of art on the wall.

Jace tries to lead me down one of the halls to our

left, but a stunning landscape done in oil catches my eye.

"Can we go see that one?" I ask, pointing at the painting in question. Jace looks longingly down the hall but eventually nods.

"Sure. Whatever you want, beautiful."

I step closer to the art, sadness hardening the pit in my stomach as I take in the delicate gradient of color. It's seamless. Beautiful. No wonder it's here on these walls.

My eyes shift to the plaque below the frame. *Ariana Swanson is a dedicated student at the Institute of Arts. At just eighteen years of age...*

I stop reading, turning away from the beautiful piece as tears threaten to break past the barrier. She's only eighteen, yet she's accomplished more than I ever will. I'm happy for her, whoever she is. Really, really happy. But I can't help but feel the crushing weight of failure now that I'm surrounded by everything I'll never be.

Slowly, I walk to Jace, hoping my face isn't showing what I'm feeling. "You wanna look at anything before we head out?"

He shrugs. "Maybe one or two things. Let's try this hallway, okay?"

I follow him dutifully, willing the ground to swallow me so I don't have to feel these wretched emotions anymore. I should be grateful for all I'm able to do. I could have lost my hand, but I didn't. I can still create beautiful art. It just might take me a while longer to gain the skills I lost.

That is, if I ever do. Maybe... maybe I should just accept reality. That I'm not good enough. That I never will be.

The thought enters my head at the same time I see it. My drawing.

My *art.*

Tears fill my eyes as I step toward the frame in a trance. I lift my hand, meaning to brush my fingertips over the crafted lines, when one of the security members steps out, an alarmed look on his face.

"Ma'am, please don't touch the art!"

Please don't touch the art. His words ring in my head. *Someone is here, making sure no one touches* my *art.*

"It's fine." Jace steps up, shooting the man a reassuring look. "She's the artist."

She's the artist. The room threatens to spin out from under me.

"Oh, my apologies." The man's cheeks redden. "So many people have been coming up to this one tonight, I've had to be extra cautious. It's a beautiful piece, ma'am."

"Thank you," I whisper, the tears falling freely now. "Thank you so much."

Jace wraps his arm over my shoulders, placing his lips to the top of my head. "It looks great up there."

"How did you do it?" I choke, my voice barely louder than a whisper. He must have paid someone to put this up here, but who?

"I didn't." He smiles, looking close to tears. "Janet entered your piece to the committee. She only told me this afternoon when she heard they had accepted it. This is all you, sunshine."

"This isn't real," I whisper, stopping just before my fingertips make contact. "Is this real, Jace?"

"Yes, my love." His lips press against my cheek. "And I don't want to say 'I told you so' or anything, but..."

My head falls back in a laugh, and I don't care who hears it. "You told me so. Have I ever told you how much I adore you?"

"Mm. Not enough," he growls, grinding against my ass. "It sounds so pretty coming from your lips, too."

A throat clears behind us, and I nearly jump out of my skin. Jace turns us so I'm facing a beautiful woman in her forties. Fifties, maybe? It's hard to tell with the work she's had done. And it looks *damn good*, too.

"I don't mean to interrupt..." Her thick English

accent is laced with boredom as she glances at Jace. She clears her throat once more, and her gaze finds mine. "I was just wondering... are you the artist?"

"Yes," I squeak, pinching my necklace between my fingers. "I am."

"I've been looking at your piece all night. Can I ask where you received your training?"

I want to dissolve under the weight of her inquisitive gaze. *She's going to find out I'm a fraud.* "The Paris College of Fine Arts. Though, I, um... technically never finished school."

When I look up, the dismissive expression I expected isn't there. She simply looks surprised. Curious, even.

"Do you mind if I ask why?"

I hold up my wrist, flinching as her gaze latches onto the silver scars. "Surfing accident. No one thought I would ever use it again, and others were waiting to fill my seat, so..."

"So they kicked you out." She nods. "What a shame."

I expect her to turn around and spit on my drawing, so when she pushes a slim black business card into my palm, I nearly fall over from surprise. The name Lisa Heathrow is painted on the front in gold foil, and there's a little inscription below that I have to squint to make out.

Talent Scout.

"I'm technically not supposed to do this..." Her voice lowers to a hush. "I'm not on company time right now, you see. But if you're interested, I'd love to talk to you about continuing your education. You've heard of the Royal Art Institute in London, yes?" The breath has left my lungs by this point, so I'm forced to nod.

She smiles, her eyes twinkling like she knows exactly what I'm thinking. "It's a shame—the way they *treated* you. I'd like to make up for their error." She winks. "That is, if you're still interested in art?"

The word *yes* is at the tip of my tongue, but I can't make myself say it. *London. A few weeks ago, I would have jumped at the opportunity. Now...*

My vision tunnels, and the only thing I'm aware of is Jace's chest pressing into my back. I can't leave. Not when I've finally found the thing that brings color to my life.

"Of course she is!" Sensing my hesitation, Jace pipes up before I have the chance to speak. "She's been in the studio nonstop these past few weeks. It's pretty much all she thinks about."

Lisa's gaze shifts to him for less than a second before it's back on me, boring into my soul. "I see. Well, you have my card. If you want to talk, I'm available at any time." She turns on her heel, shooting one last longing glance toward my drawing. "Just spectacular."

Then she's gone, leaving me to deal with the weight of the elephant-sized boulder she dropped on my chest. I'm vaguely aware of Jace fitting his fingers in mine, but all I can think about is the impossible decision I'll have to make.

Leave the love of my life, or stay and forget about my dream.

Chapter Fifteen

"YOU'RE GOING. IT'S NOT A DISCUSSION."

My veins fill with rage at Jace's insistent tone. "Like hell I am. I've finally started to find happiness here, and now you're telling me to go?"

"But you're not, Cassandra. You've just gotten comfortable living with fragments of yourself. That's not happiness. And it's certainly not the fucking life I want you to have."

I open my mouth to disagree but stop. *He's right. The bastard is right. Except he's forgetting one tiny little thing.*

"I'm happy with you," I whisper, twisting my necklace around my thumb until it purples. "When we're together, the rest of the world melts away. In those moments, I'm really, truly happy."

Jace turns his head, and the pain in his eyes makes the breath leave my lungs. "It's not enough, Cass. Not for you. We both know that." He sighs, running a hand over his beautiful face. "If you don't call Lisa, you'll wonder what could have been if you had just taken a chance. It'll tear you apart. Tear *us* apart."

"What if you forget about me?" My lip trembles, and I look away as mortification creeps up the back of my neck. *There it is. There's the real reason I don't want to go. Fear. Fear that the love of my life will move on, fear of failure. It's always fucking fear.*

Jace whips the wheel to the right, pulling off the side of the road as the car behind swerves and blows their horn. I'm about to snap at him for driving so recklessly when he grabs my face and crushes his lips to mine. His tongue teases my lower lip, pulling a mewl from deep in my chest as he expertly works his mouth with mine.

He pulls back, and I try to follow, but he holds my head firm. "Look at me, Cassandra." I can't breathe under the weight of his pained gaze, so speaking is out of the question. Luckily, he doesn't seem to want me to do much talking.

"I could never forget you," he whispers, brushing his thumb over my cheek. "I have loved you since the first time I laid eyes on you. I have worshipped you since the first word you spoke to me. I have been devoted to you ever since you held me. I love you, Cassandra. I *have* loved, and will continue to love you for as long as these tired lungs of mine will take in oxygen." He leans in, pressing his forehead to mine. "There was no woman for me before you, and there will be no one after. I'll wait as long as you need me to. I'll love you from worlds away. And when you're ready, I'll be right here where you left me."

Tears pool freely down my cheeks now. I can't think of the words to say, but by the look on Jace's face, he knows everything I'm thinking.

That I love him. That I will always love him, just as he will love me. Something as simple as distance could never come between that, and I was a fool for ever thinking it could.

"Pinky promise?" I whisper, holding the trembling digit out to him.

Jace bellows a laugh, twisting his own with mine and leaning forward to seal it with a kiss. "Pinky promise."

We drive the rest of the way to my apartment in silence, though my thoughts are anything but. I can't help but worry about what will happen to us if I go to school. Jace seems so sure we'll be okay, but how do I know he won't change his mind in a few months? With his line of work, he's surrounded by powerful, breathtaking women every day. Who's to say one of them doesn't turn his head while I'm thousands of miles away?

So lost in my misery, I only notice Jace has parked in front of my building when he pulls my door open.

"You coming, sunshine?" He holds his hand out, and I gladly take it, letting him lead me inside with shaky steps. I don't even have the energy to strip my heels off as I clamor onto the mattress. I shove my face into one of the pillows, not wanting Jace to see the tears welling.

"Cassandra?" His palm rubs soothing circles on my back, and I try to focus on the feeling of him rather than the storm brewing in my mind. "Do you want to talk about it, sunshine?"

I roll on my side, letting out a bitter laugh as I face him. "I don't feel very sunny at the moment."

His dimple deepens. "You know it's not for you, right? The nickname? He reaches out, brushing my tearstained cheek with his thumb. "It's because that's how you make me feel. It doesn't matter what happens or how shitty life gets. When I see you, my chest lights up, and all I want to do is smile. Because you're my sunshine, Cassandra. My light, my life. I hate seeing you this way," he whispers, searching my face with worry deepening his forehead. "I want to take it all away."

"You can't. Not unless you know how to ship the city of London to Florida." I giggle, my chest tightening with the reminder.

"What if I came with you? I could hold off on the expansions, and—"

"No." My voice is stern as I hold his gaze. "You're not putting your life on hold because of my insecurities, Jace. It's like you said: we'll make it through this. At the end of the day, it's only a few semesters. I can manage for a year. We made it far longer before."

Jace groans, pulling me deeper into his chest. "I'm not sure how I'm going to make it without my daily dose of Cassandra," he teases, pressing his lips to the top of my head. "We'll just have to make up for all the sex we're gonna miss before you leave."

I giggle as he rolls on top of me, pinning my head between his two muscular arms. "We should probably start now. Who knows when they'll ship you off?"

His mouth crashes against mine as I reach up, fisting my fingers through his silky hair. A moan pours from my mouth as he nips my bottom lip, pressing his hips against mine. Balancing with one arm, he grips my ankle, using it to wrap my leg around his back. There's a pop and a zipping noise, and the head of his velvety cock presses against my entrance. He slides it up and down my slit, stroking and coating the length of his cock in my arousal.

"That's my dirty girl," he coos, pushing the head lower and resting it against my back entrance. My eyes widen with a gasp as the pressure increases, and I try pushing against his chest as the feeling rises to discomfort.

He pulls away with a chuckle, putting a finger against my lips and pushing inside. "Suck," he orders, his eyes glowing with desire. "Make it nice and sloppy if you want it to go in easy."

My core tightening, I obey, swirling my tongue around his index and coating it with as much saliva as my drying mouth will allow.

"Good girl," he murmurs, pulling away and sliding his hand back to my asshole. The tip teases the tight hole before pressing inside, causing tears to spring to my eyes from the sensation. It feels wrong but weirdly amazing, especially when he teases a second finger inside.

"Fuck! Jace, it's too much," I whine, wriggling further into his palm.

"It doesn't seem that way," he coos, twisting his fingers and crooking them against my spot.

"Holy shit," I breathe, my head falling back to my shoulders. "That feels so fucking good."

"It's about to feel better," he groans, pulling away and fisting his cock. He pushes it inside my dripping cunt, coating the entire thing before pulling out and dipping to my asshole.

"Jace!" I squeal, my mouth popping as the head pushes past the tight barrier. It's not going to fit. There's no fucking way.

"Shh. Take my cock in your ass like a good little girl," Jace groans, pushing it deeper inch by inch. When his cock is halfway inside, he stops, staring down with a maniacal smirk before shoving his hips flush against me.

A scream rips from my throat as his cock threatens to split me in half. Jace moves slowly, pumping in and out and letting me get used to the sensation. When it starts to feel good and my face relaxes, he picks up the pace.

"You're so fucking tight," he breathes, every syllable choked with pleasure. "I can't fucking get enough of you."

His fingers swirl against my clit, turning the gentle thrum of pleasure into a tsunami. My entire body shakes, every nerve primed and ready to fire as the most powerful orgasm of my life crests. The sensation is too much, and when his cock pulses inside me, I topple over the edge.

Jace slows his thrusts, a matching groan pouring from his own mouth as he follows. Wave after wave of pleasure wracks through me, causing my legs to convulse uncontrollably around Jace's waist.

"Fuck, you're amazing," he breathes, slipping out of my ass with a massive grunt. "We're definitely doing that again before you leave."

"I sure hope so." I laugh, my eyelids more heavy than I ever remember them being. "That was..."

"Amazing?"

"I was gonna say earth-shattering, but I was afraid I'd sound like a broken record."

"Mm. I like yours better," he murmurs, rolling to the side and pulling me into the crook of his arm. "Did that help you realize how obsessed with you I am?"

"I guess..." I tease. "Though I might need another reminder or two."

"Trust me, I plan to give you all the reminders," he growls, his hands tightening possessively around my shoulders. "There's gonna be zero doubt in that pretty little head when I'm done with you."

"Can you say that again? It sounds so nice coming from your mouth."

Jace chuckles, leaning in and nibbling my bottom lip. "I'll say it as many times as you need, sunshine, because I'm not going anywhere. I belong to you, and I always have. Just put me out of my misery and tell me you believe it."

"I do... for tonight, at least." A smile teases my lips

as I press my forehead to his. "I'm going to fucking miss this, you know?"

"I know. But we have the rest of our lives to look forward to. Distance can't come between something meant to be, sunshine."

I close my eyes, choosing to believe him. I don't have any other choice.

Chapter Sixteen

1 year later...

"I LOVE THE WAY YOU'VE WORKED WITH THE negative space, Stone. It gives almost an... effervescent quality to her expression. Quite striking."

I give Dr. Bellum a tight-lipped smile, raising the charcoal pencil back to the canvas. Depicted in harsh black lines is a woman standing at a window, her tears flying off her face and back into her hair from the strong wind. *Longing* is the working title at the moment, and it doesn't take a genius to guess who it's dedicated to.

"Class!" Her voice rises to an authoritative screech, and I fight the urge to wince. It's happened too many times to count, but being called out in front of the rest of the students has never gotten easier. "Come take a look at Stone's piece!" she orders, thrusting a finger at my half-finished canvas. "Take note of the emotion she's managed to depict in the eyes. At first glance, you really *feel* like this woman is pining for something. I want you all to try to replicate this in your own work today. Make me *feel* something when I look at it. That's all."

Muttering breaks out as soon as she stomps away, and it's impossible to miss the nasty looks people throw my way. I don't fault them for their feelings. Hell, I was in their position when I first arrived in London. It took weeks before the professors stopped sneering at my art, and even longer before anything resembling a kind word was said. Still, I wish they would get to know me and understand that I hate being singled out as much as they do. I've yet to make a friend since I've been here, and due to the time difference, talking to my family back home has been next to impossible.

It also doesn't help that a certain brown-eyed man has been taking up every thought since I set foot on English soil.

"She's such a poser. I heard her wrist is fucked up or something. They're just singling her out because they feel sorry for her." I jerk my head to glare at the two brunettes to my right. To their credit, they have the decency to look embarrassed.

"Sorry," the one closest to me murmurs. "Didn't mean anything by it."

"Of course not." I roll my eyes, standing from my stool. I grab my pencil case and start shoving my tools in, not caring when several tips crack from the force. My chest is too tight, the room too hot. I need to get out of here.

I don't bother zipping the canvas in its case. I just shove it under my arm and hasten from the classroom as quickly as possible.

"Somewhere you need to be, Stone?" Dr. Bellum raises a perfectly manicured brow. "It must be pretty important for you to leave your piece exposed like that. You know, with the storm surging and all."

As if to emphasize her point, a boom of thunder rattles the walls. Never taking my eyes off her, I fit the canvas into its case, making sure the zipper is secure before slinging it over my shoulder.

"Sorry, Dr. Bellum. I'm just really not feeling well."

"I see." Her eyes shoot over my shoulder, scanning the room before leaning in close. "Don't let them get to you, Stone. You're better than that."

"I—thank you." I try a tight-lipped smile. "I don't intend to. I think I just need some rest. I haven't been getting much sleep lately." Or any, for that matter. Whenever I doze off, I end up falling into the same nightmare that's plagued me since the day I said goodbye to Jace at the airport. I'm in a forest, and there's a fork in the path. I always choose the left, and the outcome is always the same. A few paces down the path, and the floor drops out from under me. The darkness swallows me whole, and I fall, fall, fall...

Dr. Bellum's sigh breaks me out of my thoughts. "I know it's hard for you here, being all alone. But you only have one more semester, and then you can do anything you want. You're strong, even if you have a hard time believing it, and I want to make sure you succeed here." She reaches out, squeezing my shoulder with a motherly affection. "Go get some rest. You can finish this assignment when you're feeling better."

"Thanks, Dr. Bellum. I'll do that." As the words come out, I'm not so sure they're the truth. Another student steps up to the desk, and I use the distraction to hurry from the room. I walk the mile and a half to the resident building, trying not to look at the groups of smiling faces passing me on the sidewalk.

Before I head to my room, I stop by the front desk to see if any packages have arrived for me. When we realized phone calls were nearly impossible with our schedules and time change, Jace came up with the idea to write each other letters in addition to texting. It sounded cheesy at first, but the weekly installments have helped fill the void that his absence creates. Sometimes, I pore over his old letters when I can't sleep, and I can almost pretend he's in bed with me, whispering those words in my ear.

"Hey, Laurie." I grin at the mousy-haired student behind the desk. "You got any letters for me today?"

"Cass!" Her smile splits her face from ear to ear, and I swear she's about to fall out of her seat as she thrusts a letter in my direction. "I've been waiting all day to give it to you. It got here during art history."

"Thanks, Laurie. My last class totally wiped me out, so I'm gonna take a nap."

She gives me a wave goodbye, but as I turn for the stairs, I swear she whispers something under her breath.

"What?" I whip around, a brow raised in her direction.

"Hm?" She feigns a look of innocence. "Something wrong?"

"No... It just sounded like you said 'doubt it.'"

"Me? I didn't say anything. Enjoy your nap!" She waves again and disappears behind the desk.

Okay...

Shaking my head, I climb the stairs to my floor, then hasten down the hallway to my room. Slamming the door closed with my back, I tear into the envelope, unable to wait a moment longer to see Jace's words.

I frown at the single piece of paper stuffed inside. Usually, Jace's letters go on for pages, and it doesn't even look like he wrote on both sides. *Oh my God, is this a breakup letter?*

I open it up, confusion muddling my racing thoughts as I stare at the single sentence scrawled along the top.

It's good to see you're still wearing that old necklace.

A chuckle sounds from across the room, and I jolt, dropping the letter as I leap backward in fright.

"What the hell!" My eyes pop as my very real, very sexy best friend stands from where he lounged on my couch. "Jace, what are you doing he—"

I don't even get the rest of the sentence out before his mouth is on mine, kissing me with such fervor I'm sure we'll both burst into flames. His hands grip my ass, hoisting me up so I can wrap my legs around his hips. He takes my bottom lip between his teeth, letting out a sound that sends a surge of heat straight to my core.

"Jace," I whisper. "How did you—"

"I couldn't stay away. I needed to have you," he mutters, kissing along my cheeks and forehead.

"But your business deal—"

"Will happen one way or another. It's not what

matters right now, sunshine. I'm just so sorry I wasn't here sooner." His lips find mine again, and I can't think of a single other reason to fight this. He's finally here, with me, where I've wanted him.

"Thank you," I whisper happily, taking in deep lungfuls of his scent. "You already made it up to me, though."

"What?" he asks, running a rough palm across my hair with all the gentleness in the world. "How's that, sunshine?"

"By being here." I tell him, tears beginning to well up my vision, "I was worried... When I saw the letter, I thought you were breaking up with me."

Jace's jaw twitches as he fists a hand at the back of my head. "Don't you ever think that again. I promised you I'd wait for you, Cassandra. Pinky promised, even." I open my mouth to speak, but the look Jace shoots me has my words dying in my throat. "I gave you my *word*, Cassandra. I keep my word. Just like I'm going to keep you for the rest of my life. As long as it's still what you want, too."

"I do. But I'm scared we'll end up like every other good thing in my life because I ruin those things. Or worse, the world ruins them for me," I whisper, cradling my wrist against Jace's sturdy chest.

"You might have lost a lot of things you cared about in this life, but I don't plan on being one of those," Jace murmurs. "Now stop worrying so much and kiss me, woman."

I laugh and press my lips to his, fisting my fingers in his hair as he walks us to the bedroom. Being safe in his arms again feels like a dream, one I have no intention of waking from.

Placing me tenderly on the mattress, he crouches at the foot of the bed, his chin resting between my thighs. The look on his face is full of wonder, and I'd give my good hand at this moment to know what he's thinking.

"God, I missed you," he whispers, his voice choked with an emotion I haven't heard before. If my drawing was the physical embodiment of longing, his tone would be the verbal one.

"I missed you. Endlessly. It's all I could think about. That, and your letters." I reach up, twisting my necklace around my pinky finger. "I wanted so badly for you to visit, but I... I couldn't bring myself to ask you."

"I wish you would have." His face is tortured, no doubt running through all the nights spent apart. "I would have been here on the next flight."

"I know. And that's half the problem. You deserve to live your life, too, Jace. You shouldn't be following me around the world, just like I shouldn't have to follow you. It's not fair to either of us."

His expression darkens. "You still don't get it, do you?"

"What?"

"My life is nothing without you in it, Cassandra. All the money, the fancy cars, and fame. It means fucking nothing if I'm not by your side. If I'm not there to watch you achieve your dreams." He shakes his head, his jaw ticking. "I was an idiot last year. The day we said goodbye at the airport... I knew in my gut that it was the biggest mistake of my life."

His eyes find mine, and the emotion swirling takes all the breath from my lungs. "I'm not going to make it again. Fuck the expansion. If the investors want it so badly, they can make it happen without me being their frontman." His palms find my thighs, gripping me with a desperate kind of pressure. "I need you, Cassandra. Let me fucking have you."

I stay silent for a while, drinking in everything he's telling me. He loves me. He wants to support me, to make sure I find my own light in this world. Why didn't I understand it last year?

"Okay."

It's barely a whisper, but Jace leaps with such joy, you would have thought I screamed it. He lunges forward, his hands encasing my head as we topple backward to the mattress.

"I love you, Cassandra," he breathes, crushing his mouth to mine. "God, do I love you."

"You're in luck, Mr. Maddox," I whisper, my lids lowering as Jace works his way down my neck. "Because I love you, too."

"Good," he chokes, his fingers tightening on my waist. "Now say it while you're coming on my cock."

2 years later...

"YOU CAN'T BE LATE TO YOUR OWN SHOWING, sunshine." Jace chuckles, crossing his arms where he's leaning on the doorframe. I swipe the crusty black line with my pinky finger, willing my hands to stop shaking so I can get my eyeliner somewhat decent.

"I wish Kasey was here to do this for me," I groan, giving up and deciding to just go with some mascara and blush. "Whose idea was it to move to another country, anyway?"

"Yours, I believe." He laughs, pushing off the frame and stopping behind me. His hands find my waist, and he presses a tender kiss against my neck. "You just had to go and be so brilliantly talented."

My belly warms as his words pour over me. I still

can't believe we're living in London. Or that Dr. Bellum was able to get me this position at the gallery. It took months, but today, I'm finally showing my collection of charcoal drawings at the Gallery of Fine Arts.

"I'm so nervous, Jace. What if everyone hates it?"

"They're not going to," he asserts, tightening his grip. "And if they do, fuck them. They don't know what they're talking about."

"I think you might be a tad biased." I giggle, turning around to face him. "You're my fiancé. You're supposed to say things like that."

"I'm not just saying it. I mean it." He swats my ass and pulls away slightly. "Come on, gorgeous. The cab is waiting downstairs."

"Okay."

I follow him to the curb where a white Fiat is waiting, my heart lodged in my throat. I haven't eaten anything all day, and I'm starting to regret pouring the smoothie Jace made me down the drain. My knees are shaking loud enough for people across the street to hear.

"Where to?"

"Fine Arts Gallery." Jace pipes up with a smile. "She has a showing tonight."

"Oh? Congratulations." The man grunts, pulling onto the main road. "That's quite an accomplishment."

"Thank you," I murmur, my face heating. I still haven't gotten used to people complimenting me on my accomplishments, but Jace loves telling anyone who will listen about my art, so it gets less embarrassing every time.

Jace places his hand on my bare thigh, giving me a gentle squeeze of encouragement. "I'm so proud of you," he whispers, his eyes shining with the same sentiment.

"I love you." I grin, leaning so my head rests on his sturdy shoulder. Jace looks delicious today in a tan fitted suit, and it's taking everything in me not to jump his bones in the cab.

As if knowing my thoughts, a chuckle rumbles in his chest, and his fingertips creep toward my core. I shoot him an alarmed look but don't care to stop him as he makes contact with my clit.

"I'm so glad you stopped wearing those awful things," he murmurs, swirling the nub gently.

"Kinda hard to when you rip every pair I try to buy," I whisper, biting my lip to suppress a moan as Jace presses the pad of his thumb inside me. A buzzing sound breaks me out of my spell, and I reach in my bag for my phone while Jace continues teasing me.

"Jace!" I hiss. "It's Ethan."

"Mm. Tell him I said hello," he murmurs, swirling his finger against my walls.

"Men." I roll my eyes as I pull the phone to my ear. "Ethan, what's up?"

"Just wanted to congratulate you on your show-ing... Wait, shit! That's still tonight, right?" His voice drips with exhaustion, and I can't help but smile.

"It is. Thank you," I say, unable to help the short-ness in my tone. I can't fucking concentrate while Jace is inside me, and the asshole knows it based on that devious smirk. Just then, a high-pitched scream rings in the bathroom, and Ethan lets out a curse.

"Everything okay?"

"Yeah. Fuck me, I just woke the baby up." A smack sounds through the phone, and I'm pretty sure he just face-palmed. "I'm sorry, Cass, I gotta go. Good luck tonight. You're gonna kill it!" The line goes dead, and I can't help but let out a relieved sigh.

Jace's lips brush the shell of my ear, and I shudder. "Baby problems?"

"Was it the ear-piercing crying that gave it away?"

His chest rumbles with a chuckle as he pulls his hand away, resting it instead on my lower abdomen.

"I can't wait until you let me put a few of them inside you." His voice is husky, causing a ball of desire to unwind in my core.

"I think we should focus on the wedding before we bring babies into the equation," I say, rolling my eyes even though the words feel like lies out in the open.

"Hmm. That's not what you said last night while you were creaming my cock," he whispers, tightening his fingers on my thigh.

"Jace!" I hiss, eyeing the driver not two feet from us. "He's literally right there."

"And? I bet he understands." A low chuckle rings out, proving Jace's point while my face heats with mortification.

"I'm so sorry, sir," I grumble, elbowing Jace lightly in the ribs.

"It's okay." He chortles. "We're here, by the way."

"Oh. Right." Jace cackles while I follow him out of the cab, holding his arm for balance. "Thank you so much."

"Good luck tonight." He winks, giving us a wave before peeling away from the curb.

"After you, sunshine." Jace's hand rests on my lower back, giving me a surge of confidence as we make our way up the stone steps to the gallery.

The place is packed. Dozens of people filter around the gallery halls, taking in each of my drawings with a critical eye. With all the different faces, there's one woman who I can't seem to take my eyes off. I feel like I know her, not because I've ever met her, but due to the amount of times I've seen her self-portraits. *Sylvia Fox.*

I cling to Jace's arm, hoping a surge of bravery will

replace the fear in my veins. She's the most talented portrait artist of this decade, and the fact that she's looking at *my* drawings is paralyzing.

"You know her?" Jace asks, tipping his chin in the direction of her snow white braid. "Wanna go say hi?"

"I don't know…" Jace doesn't seem to hear me as he leads me in her direction. "Jace, I really don't think she wants to talk to me."

"You're the artist. She came to your show. Of course she does." He rolls his eyes, stopping us a few feet from where she stands, inspecting a portrait of a couple embracing underwater.

He taps me, and I clear my throat. "Hi, Ms. Fox. I don't mean to disturb you, but—"

She whips to face me, the cold expression on her face stopping the words in my throat.

"Yes? How can I help you?"

With Jace at my side, I somehow find the bravery to speak. "I saw you looking at my piece. I just wanted to introduce myself. I'm—"

"Cassandra Stone. Of course." The chilliness in her gaze washes away. "I've been anxious to meet you, Ms. Stone. Your drawings have really touched me." A smile tugs at her thin lips, adding a bit of warmth to her serious demeanor. "You're quite an enigma in the art circles. People tell me you almost lost your hand?"

"That's right," I nod, waiting for a familiar twinge of pain when I think about it.

But it never comes.

"Astounding." She nods like it's been decided for me. "Well, Ms. Stone, I look forward to see what you create in the future. Here." She presses a silver business card in my palm. "Give me a call if you want to work together in the future."

With that, she's gone, whirling out of the gallery with dozens of envious eyes trailing after her.

"Jace?" I whisper, my eyes locked on the slim card. "Did that just happen?"

"You bet your sexy ass it did." He wraps his arms around me, squeezing all the air from my lungs. "I'm so proud of you, my brilliant, brilliant artist."

I don't know what to say. If someone had told me this would happen to me two years ago, I would have laughed in their face. Now that it's reality... I don't even know what to do.

One thing is for sure. I never would have gotten here if I didn't have my Greek god of a fiancé behind me the whole way. He's helped me piece myself back together and been the light in my never-ending darkness. He's my home.

"Jace?"

"Yes, sunshine?"

"I fucking love you."

Jace laughs, the sound reverberating off the walls of the gallery. "Cassandra?"

"Yes, handsome?"

"I fucking love you more."

He crushes his mouth to mine, and the rest of the world fades away. His lips, his scent, and his love are the only things left in the space between us. Even the air leaves my lungs, but I welcome the sensation.

Jace Maddox is all I need.

Did you miss Ethan & Amelia's story? Grab Time & Tide!

About the Author

Mindy Paige was born and raised in Florida. She started writing at a young age. After getting her degree in botany, she decided to pursue her dream of being an author. Her debut romance novel, Time and Tide, was written while finishing her senior year of college.

If not writing or reading, Mindy can usually be found playing with her dogs, tending to her plants, watching reality television with her boyfriend, or painting.

Don't miss out on release news and giveaways; join Mindy's newsletter!

Printed in Great Britain
by Amazon